THE ITALIAN'S
ONE-NIGHT BABY

THE ITALIAN'S
ONE-NIGHT BABY

BY

LYNNE GRAHAM

First published in Great Britain 2017
By Mills & Boon, an imprint of HarperCollins*Publishers*
1 London Bridge Street, London, SE1 9GF

Large Print edition 2017

LP

ISBN: 978-0-263-07120-7

Our policy is to use papers that are natural, renewable
and recyclable products and made from wood grown
in sustainable forests. The logging and manufacturing
processes conform to the legal environmental regulations
of the country of origin.

Printed and bound in Great Britain
by CPI Antony Rowe, Chippenham, Wiltshire

My husband, Michael,
for his constant support and kindness
over the years.

CHAPTER ONE

RIO BENEDETTI SET his even, white teeth together hard and suppressed a very rude word as his god-father cheerfully chatted on about his plans to entertain his unexpected guest. Beppe Sorrentino was a naïve man, trusting and generous to a fault, not at all the sort of man to suspect his self-invited guest of a hidden agenda. Luckily he had a godson like Rio, determined to shield the older man from anyone trying to take him for a ride.

Rio, the billionaire veteran of many triumphant wins in the business world and a man cynically unimpressed by women, knew he had to proceed with discretion because Ellie Dixon had powerful, wealthy friends, and most important, she was the sister of Polly, the current queen of Dharia—a country which rejoiced in oil wealth. Even worse, on paper at least, Ellie was impressive. Nobody knew that better than Rio, who had met her at his friend Rashad's wedding to her sister Polly. She was a beautiful, intelligent and hard-working doctor. But saintly Dr Ellie's profile took a fast nosedive if you had her past history exhaustively checked. At best Rio knew her to be a thief and a gold-digger, at worst she could be the kind of doctor who befriended the elderly to persuade them to change their wills in her favour.

Ellie had had a disciplinary action brought against her at work after an elderly patient had died endowing Ellie with all her worldly goods. Not surprisingly, the old lady's nephew had filed a complaint. But then there had been indications that Ellie might have an unseemly lust for money earlier than that, Rio acknowledged, thinking of the section in the investigative report relating to her grandmother's diamond brooch. The valuable brooch should've gone to Ellie's uncle but Ellie had somehow acquired it instead, causing much family bitterness.

No, nothing about Ellie Dixon was straight-forward, not least her surprising approach to his godfather in a letter in which she had asked to visit because Beppe had apparently once known her late mother.

Of course, it was equally possible that Rio himself was the actual target in Dr Ellie's sights, he conceded with a certain amount of cynical satisfaction at that idea. Perhaps Ellie hadn't realised just how very rich he was at the wedding and, knowing where he lived, had come up with this vague connection as an excuse to visit his godfather, Beppe. Women, after all, had often gone to quite extraordinary lengths to try to reel him in, and he was as slick as an eel when it came to avoiding commitment.

He refused to think about what had happened with Ellie at Rashad's wedding because Rio did not believe in reconstructing unpleasant past events. With women he was very much a 'hit it and quit it' kind of guy. He didn't do serious and he didn't do long-term. Why would he? He was thirty years old, rich as sin and very good-looking and his female options were so many and varied that, had he wanted to and without effort, he could have slept with a different woman every night of the year. So, if he was Dr Ellie's target she was in for a severe disillusionment. In any case, the woman was an absolute shrew with a streak of violence, he recalled sardonically.

'You're very quiet, Rio…' Beppe remarked. 'You don't approve of Annabel's daughter visiting, do you?'

'Why would you think that?' Rio parried, surprised that the older man had seen through his tolerant front.

Beppe simply grinned. He was a small man with greying hair and rather round in shape. Perched in his favourite armchair, he had the cheerful air of a playful gnome and Rio's shrewd dark eyes softened the instant they settled on him because Beppe Sorrentino was as dear to Rio as any father could have been.

'I saw you wince when I mentioned how disappointed I was that Ellie wouldn't agree to stay here in my home as my guest. She's a very frank young lady. She said she wouldn't be comfortable because she doesn't know me and would prefer to stay at the hotel.'

'It wouldn't be comfortable for you either to have her here. You're not used to having guests,' Rio pointed out, for Beppe had been a childless widower for almost twenty years and lived a very quiet and peaceful life in his family *palazzo* a few miles outside Florence.

'I know but I get bored,' Beppe admitted abruptly. 'Bored and lonely. No, don't look at me like that, Rio. You visit plenty. But, Ellie's visit will be stimulating. A fresh face, different company.'

'*Dio mio...*' Rio rhymed thoughtfully. 'Why are you so reluctant to tell me anything about Ellie's mother and yet so excited about her daughter coming here?'

Beppe's rounded face locked down so fast it was like a vault sliding shut and his dark eyes evaded his godson's. 'It's not something I can discuss with you, Rio. Please don't take that the wrong way.'

Rio's even, white teeth gritted again. He had

even considered the idea that in some way Ellie could be engaged in an attempt to blackmail his godfather about some dark secret, but even optimistic Beppe would hardly look forward so happily to the visit of a blackmailer. Furthermore Rio couldn't imagine that Beppe *had* any dark secrets because he was the most open, transparent personality Rio had ever known. Yet Beppe had known great unhappiness and loss in his private life. His delightful wife, Amalia, had given birth to a stillborn son and had then suffered a severe stroke. From then on right up until her death, Beppe's wife had endured precarious health and the confinement of a wheelchair. Beppe, however, had remained utterly devoted to his beloved Amalia and, although now pushing sixty, had evinced not the smallest desire to meet another woman.

Rio, in strong comparison, had never been open or trusting with other human beings. He was naturally suspicious and naturally complex. He had been abandoned in a dumpster at birth, born to a heroin-addicted mother and an unknown father and he had spent his formative years in an orphanage until Amalia Sorrentino took an interest in him. Through Amalia he had met her kindly husband, his benefactor. He knew very well that he owed almost everything he had become and everything he had achieved to the man seated by the fireside who had first recognised his intelligence and there was little he would not have done to protect Beppe from any potential harm. And Rio was absolutely convinced that in some way Ellie Dixon was a harmful threat.

Evil temptress? Gold-digging harpy? Hard-nosed feminist? Thief? Scam artist with the elderly? At Rashad's wedding, he had been treated to giggly, amusing Ellie and enraged Ellie. He had also been led down the garden path right to the door of his hotel room and then assaulted. He hadn't forgotten the experience. He hadn't forgiven it either. Insults lingered with Rio. For too many years of his life he had been a nameless orphan, bullied and abused and dismissed as unimportant. And Ellie Dixon had cut him down to size as effectively as the most terrifying nun at the orphanage, Sister Teresa, who had struggled to overcome Rio's stormy and essentially vengeful temperament.

No, Rio wasn't the forgiving and forgetting sort. He still occasionally dreamt about Ellie twirling on the dance floor in her diaphanous green dress, her glorious mane of red curls tumbling round her animated face, and he would remember how he had felt and it stung him like salt in an open wound. He had felt that night that he would die if he didn't have her. Lust multiplied by wine and wedding fervour, he dismissed now with still-gritted teeth. Now all he had to do was sit back and wait for Ellie and her character of many divergent colours to emerge into the unforgiving glare of daylight...

So, would she be the temptress, the prim doctor, the clever academic or the friendly, casual tourist? And just how long would it take for Rio to find out what her game was?

Whatever, it was still game on...

* * *

Ellie surveyed the vast cache of clothing in sheer wonderment.

'Yes, your pressie has arrived,' she confirmed to her sister Polly, with the phone tucked in her nape. 'What on earth were you thinking of?'

'I know you don't do shopping, so I did it for you,' Polly responded cheerfully. 'You need a holiday wardrobe for Italy and I bet you haven't had the time to buy anything... Am I right?'

On that score, Polly was right but Ellie, picking up a floaty white sundress with a designer label, was gobsmacked by her sister's generosity. Correction, her sister's embarrassingly *endless* generosity. 'Well, I'm really more of a "jeans and tee" sort of girl,' she reminded her sibling. 'In fact, I think the last time I put on a sundress was when I was visiting you. You know I'm very, very grateful, Polly, but I wish you wouldn't spend so much money on me. I'm a junior doctor, I'm not living on the breadline—'

'I'm your big sister and it gives me a lot of pleasure to buy you things,' Polly told her unanswerably. 'Come on, Ellie… Don't be stiff and stuffy about this. We never got much in the way of pressies and treats growing up and I want to share my good fortune with you. It's only money. Don't make it change things between us—'

But it *was* changing things, Ellie thought, suppressing a sigh. She might always have been the kid sister in their duo but she had also always been the leader and she couldn't help missing that familiarity and her sister, who now lived half the world away in Dharia. Polly didn't turn to her for advice any more. Polly no longer needed her in the same way. Polly had Rashad now, and a gorgeous little son, and unless Ellie was very much mistaken there would soon be another little royal prince or princess on the horizon. Her sister also had a pair of adoring grandparents in Dharia, who had welcomed her into her late father's side of the family with loving enthusiasm.

And that was why Ellie was travelling out to Italy clutching the emerald ring gifted to their by her late mother, Annabel, whom she had never known. Annabel had died in a hospice after a long illness while her daughters were raised by their grandmother. Ellie's mother had left behind three rings in separate envelopes for her daughters.

That there were *three* envelopes had been the first shock because until that moment Ellie and Polly had not realised that they had another sister, younger than they were, raised apart from them and most probably in council care. A sister, Lucy, completely unknown to them. In each envelope their mother had written the name of each girl's father.

Polly had flown out to Dharia to research her background in the hope of finding her father, only to discover that he had died before she was even born, but she had been compensated for that loss by the existence of welcoming, loving grandparents. In the midst of that family reunion, Polly had married Rashad, the king of Dharia, and become a queen. As soon as she had married she and Rashad had hired a private detective to try to locate Lucy but the search had been hampered by officialdom's rules of confidentiality.

Ellie had received an emerald ring along with two male names on a scrap of writing paper... Beppe and Vincenzo Sorrentino. She assumed that one of those men was her father and she already knew that one of them was dead. She knew absolutely nothing else and wasn't even sure she really *wanted* to know what kind of entanglement her mother had contrived to have with two men, who were brothers. If that made her a prude, too bad, she thought ruefully. She couldn't help her own nature, could she? And she didn't have unrealistic expectations about what she might discover about her paternity in Italy. Neither man might have been her father, in which case she would simply have to accept living with her ignorance. But the discovery of *any* kind of relative would be welcome, she conceded sadly, because since Polly's marriage she had missed having a family within reach.

At the same time she asked herself why she still cherished that idealistic image of 'family,' because the grandmother who had raised her and Polly had not been a warm or loving person and her mother's brother, her uncle Jim, had been downright horrible even when they were children. In fact, recalling how the older man had treated her in the aftermath of his own mother's death made Ellie flame up with angry resentment, which made her wonder if she would *ever* share that sad story with Polly. Probably not, because Polly preferred only to see the good in people.

In the same way Polly had blithely declared that her marriage would change nothing between the sisters but, in fact, it had changed *everything*. Ellie didn't even like to phone her sister too often because she was very aware that Polly had far more pressing and important commitments as a wife, a mother and a queen. Ellie loved to visit Dharia, as well, but the long flights would eat up a weekend off and she often spent her leave simply catching up on sleep because junior doctors routinely had to work very long hours. At her most recent training rotation she had been working at a hospice and her duties and her patients had drained her both mentally and emotionally.

Indeed as she packed the new wardrobe Polly had had delivered to her into a pair of suitcases Ellie was too weary even to examine the garments and belatedly very grateful that her sister had saved her from an exhaustive shopping trip. No doubt she would look a lot fancier and more feminine in clothing Polly had picked than she would in anything she would have chosen for herself, she thought ruefully, because she had never been interested in fashion.

Far more importantly, Ellie was much more excited about even the slight prospect that she might find her father in Italy. Even Polly, with whom Ellie had played it very cool and cynical on that topic, had no real idea how much Ellie longed to find a father at the end of the Italian trail.

Two days later, Ellie walked down the stairs of the small rural hotel she had chosen and was shown out to a delightful three-sided patio, which was festooned with flowers and overlooked a rolling section of the green, vine-covered Tuscan landscape. She breathed in the fresh air with a smile of pure pleasure and relaxed for the first time in many weeks.

Tomorrow she had an appointment to meet Beppe Sorrentino at his home, but today she was free to explore her surroundings and that lack of an actual to-do list was an unadulterated luxury. She settled down at her solo table, smoothing down the light cotton skirt and top she wore in mint green, only momentarily thinking that the uneven handkerchief hems Polly loved were very impractical. Fashion isn't about practicality, she could hear her sister telling her squarely, and she smiled fondly as a brimming cup of cappuccino coffee arrived along with a basket of pastries.

Ellie powered through her usual work schedule on snatched coffee pick-me-ups and the fresh cappuccino was glorious, as was the croissant, which melted in her appreciative mouth. Indeed it was as she was brushing tiny flakes of pastry from her lips that a tall, dark silhouette blotted out her wonderful view. She blinked behind her sunglasses, supposing it was too much to have hoped that she would be allowed to have the patio and the view all to herself. After all, it was a very small hotel but still a hotel and naturally there would be other guests.

A liquid burst of Italian greeted the new arrival, whom Ellie could not yet see because of the sunlight. The waiter seemed to be falling over himself in his eagerness to greet the man, which probably meant he was a regular or a local, she thought idly. He responded in equally fast and fluent Italian and there was something about that voice, that dark chocolate honeyed drawl, that struck a dauntingly familiar note with Ellie and she paled, dismissing that jolt of familiarity with brisk common sense. After all, it couldn't be the same man, simply couldn't be! *He* lived in the city of Florence and she was miles outside the city, staying in a village hotel convenient to Beppe Sorrentino's home. No, it absolutely couldn't be the male who had totally destroyed her enjoyment of her sister's wedding festivities and left her filled with self-loathing and regret. Even fate couldn't be cruel enough to sentence her to a second meeting with Rio Benedetti, her worst nightmare cloaked in male flesh.

'*Buongiorno*, Ellie...' Rio murmured silkily as he yanked out the vacant chair at her table and sat down.

Shock, mortification and anger seized Ellie all at once. 'What the heck are you doing here?' she demanded baldly before she could think better of such revealing aggression.

Rio Benedetti angled his handsome dark head back, his dazzling dark golden eyes veiled by his ridiculously long black lashes. He had blue-black hair that he wore cropped short but the strands still revealed a striking tendency to curl, which gave him a tousled, sexy aspect. He had beautiful eyes, a lean straight nose and bone structure that belonged in an oil painting of a dark angel. He smiled back at her in complete silence.

That fast, Ellie wanted to slap Rio all over again and tell him what she thought of him even though she had already done that two years earlier. He was gorgeous and he *knew* it, a hanging offence in her list of the attributes of a decent man. In reality she had never met such a stunningly good-looking male as Rio and when she had, she had caved as fast as a brick shed built on sand foundations, she recalled with an inner shudder of revulsion.

Why? she still asked herself occasionally, because that kind of impulsive recklessness was not Ellie, not her way with men, not her style, nor even how she was prepared to behave. Unfortunately she hadn't counted on meeting a Rio Benedetti blessed with such extreme magnetism, intelligence and charm. At least that was how she had excused herself for having very nearly succumbed to a one-night stand that had no prospect of any future but she was still ashamed of her misjudgement, still unable to forget that awful moment when that hotel bedroom door opened and she saw what was already waiting on his bed for him…

Rio didn't want to smile. He didn't want to fake it, he wanted to glower at her, and he hadn't planned to sit down either. No, standing over her, intimidating her with his much greater height had been his intention. But then he had seen her and all bets were suddenly off. Watching the tip of that little pink tongue chase stray flakes of pastry from her full pink lips had been more than his libido could bear. And his libido rode him like a runaway express train around Ellie Dixon, his arousal enforcing the necessity of sitting down to conceal his condition. What was he? An uncontrollably horny fifteen-year-old again? Dark colour lined his hard cheekbones. Regardless of the fact that he disliked and distrusted Ellie, she was a real beauty with skin as translucent as creamy porcelain, luminous eyes as green as any emerald and a wealth of tumbling Titian curls. Although smaller than average height, she had stupendous sexy curves matched with a tiny waist. Her proportions were truly breathtaking.

Rio had been sexually entranced with Ellie Dixon from the instant he'd laid eyes on her and when he had been rejected for the first time in his adult life the bite of that experience had stayed with him. Ellie had returned to his hotel with him the night of her sister's wedding but, on the very brink of intimacy, it had all gone wrong. In departing, Ellie had slapped him and insulted him. Rio gritted his teeth at the recollection of that experience. Far too many people had treated Rio with contempt when he was younger for him to easily overlook that kind of slur.

'What do you think I'm doing here?' Rio enquired smoothly, turning her own question back on her.

Ellie shrugged a shoulder and concentrated on her cappuccino. She didn't even want to speak to him but could she be *that* rude? After all, he was her brother-in-law's best friend and she liked Polly's husband. 'Did Rashad tell you I was going to be here and ask you to check up on me?' she asked abruptly, thinking that that was just the sort of protective thing Rashad would do, believing that he was doing her a favour when she was staying in an unfamiliar place.

'No. I don't think Rashad knows you're in Italy,' Rio admitted.

'So, I don't need to be polite, then,' Ellie assumed with satisfaction, reaching out for another pastry.

A sizzling smile slashed Rio's wide, sensual mouth. 'No, neither of us need be polite.'

That smile of his engulfed Ellie like a blast of sun on a wintry day and she wanted to turn into it and smile back in reward. Suppressing that reaction took the exercising of several seconds of strained self-control. But Rio had still won in one sense because although she didn't return the smile her whole body was reacting to him in the most unnerving manner. Her teeth gritted as she recognised the stinging tightness of her nipples and the warm liquid feeling between her thighs. He could tempt her wretched hormones with just a glance and she hated him for having that much power over her treacherous body. Had she no pride? And after what he had done to her, had he not a single honourable streak in his character?

'So, if we don't need to be polite...' Ellie hesitated only for a second before giving him a very honest response. 'Go away, Rio.'

A very faint stab of bewilderment penetrated

Rio's sharp-as-a-tack brain. He had decided in the absence of any other evidence that Ellie had most probably dreamt up some vague link between her late mother and his godfather purely to gain fresh access to *him*. And either she was now playing ridiculously hard to get in the hope of stoking his interest...*or*, he was actually nothing whatsoever to do with her reasons for visiting Tuscany.

'I don't believe in coincidences,' Rio asserted, his sculpted lips compressing as his coffee arrived along with the hotel owner, who lingered to exchange greetings both with Rio and Ellie.

'I don't believe in coincidences either,' Ellie told Rio with a freezing smile once they were alone again. 'I mean, it was bad enough meeting you at Polly's wedding...but *this*—this is overkill of the worst kind—'

'Is it really?' Rio was fearful of getting frostbite from that smile, marvelling that Ellie could dare to treat him with such disdain, and his strong and aggressive jawline clenched hard.

'Yes, I do appreciate that this is your home

country but I can't believe we're running into each other again…accidentally,' she admitted.

'And you would be correct. My presence here is no accident,' Rio confirmed softly as he sipped his espresso, contriving to look relaxed.

But Ellie knew he wasn't relaxed. Rio had certain tells. She had picked up on them at Polly's wedding. His eyes were veiled, his jawline tight, his fingers too braced round the tiny cup he held. Rio was tense, *very* tense, and she wondered why and then she wondered why she would even care. He was the man whore she had almost slept with, and she was very grateful that she had found him out for what he was *before* she shared a bed with him. Having carefully ensured that she'd never visited Dharia when he was also visiting, there was no reason for her to waste further words or time on him.

'So, why are you calling on me? And how did you know where I was staying?'

'I want to know what you're doing here in Tuscany,' Rio informed her flatly without answering her questions.

'I'm on holiday,' Ellie told him with a roll of her fine eyes.

'I don't think that is the complete truth, Ellie,' Rio scoffed with a sardonic smile.

'Well, it's the only truth you're likely to get out of me,' Ellie responded as she stood up, her fine-boned features stiff with restraint and annoyance. 'It's not as though we're friends.'

Rio sprang upright with fluid grace. At her sister's wedding, his grace of movement had been one of the first things she'd noticed about him: he stalked like an animal on the hunt, all power and strength and purpose. 'Would you like to be friends?' he asked lethally.

Ellie stiffened where she stood, quick to pick up on the husky erotic note edging his enquiry. 'No. I'm very choosy about the men I call friends,' she declared with deliberate cool, not caring whether Rio assumed that she meant friends with benefits or not.

Heat flared like a storm warning in Rio's dark golden eyes. 'You chose me in Dharia,' he reminded her with satisfaction.

Ellie's hand tingled as she remembered slapping him hard that night. It occurred to her that a fist would have been better and less forgettable on his terms. She was outraged that he could remind her of that night when in her opinion, had he had any morals at all, he should've been thoroughly ashamed of how their short-lived flirtation had ended. But then Rio Benedetti was a shameless sort of guy, arrogant and selfish and promiscuous. That he should also be as hot as hellfire enraged her sense of justice.

'But I wouldn't touch you even with gloves on now,' Ellie traded without skipping a beat and, turning on her heel, she walked back into the hotel.

'Ellie... We will have this conversation whether you like it or not,' Rio ground out with a low-pitched derision that nonetheless cut through the sunlit silence like a knife. 'Walking away won't save you from it.'

'And you coming over all caveman and beating your chest won't get you anywhere,' Ellie murmured cuttingly over a slim shoulder. 'I've never been one of those women whose heart beats a little faster when a man turns domineering.'

'But then you hadn't met me,' Rio imparted in a raw undertone.

'And once met, never forgotten,' Ellie traded, saccharine sweet laced with acid. 'I live and learn, Rio… *Don't you?*'

With that final scornful comment, Ellie vanished into the cool gloom of the hotel. Rio wanted to smash something, break something, *shout*. It reminded him that that was yet another trait he loathed in his quarry. She got under his skin, set his teeth on edge, made him feel *violent*. And that wasn't him, had never been him around women, where he was usually the essence of complete cool and sophistication in his approach. At the same time Ellie sent disturbing cascades of sexual imagery tumbling through his brain. He would picture Ellie in his bed, all spread out and satisfied, Ellie on her knees, Ellie across the bonnet of his favourite sports car. *Troppa fantasia…* too much imagination, again a trait that only she awakened, and annoying. After all, he wasn't sex-starved, anything but. Possibly he had become a little bored with easily available women, who clung and flattered and pawed him like a trophy to be shown off, he reasoned impatiently.

But he didn't want Ellie Dixon except in the most basic male way and he had no intention of doing anything about the effect she had on him. And she might live and learn but she had still to learn that he didn't let *anyone* walk away from him before he had finished speaking. Without further hesitation, Rio strode indoors.

Ellie closed the door of her room behind her and leant back against it in a panic that nobody who knew her would ever have credited. Her heart was racing and she was sweating. She straightened her slim shoulders and stomped into the en-suite to wash her hands and put herself back into her usual calm, collected state of mind. She did not allow men to rattle her. She had never allowed men to rattle her.

But two years back, Rio Benedetti had pierced

her shell and hurt her, she acknowledged grudgingly. He had contrived what no man before him had contrived and she had almost made a fool of herself over him. Wouldn't he just love to know that? Ellie grimaced. A man she had known for only a few hours had deprived her of her wits and defences and come close to ridding her of her virginity with her full collusion. And then he had unlocked his bedroom door and she had seen that his hotel bed was already occupied by not one, no, not one but *two* giggling naked women, twin sisters she had noticed at the wedding. Appalled, she had stepped back.

And Rio had smirked and laughed as if it was of no consequence that two other women were already waiting to entertain him. Even in retrospect she marvelled that she had slapped him instead of kicking him somewhere unforgivable because she had been devastated by that revealing glimpse of his lifestyle, his habits, his lack of scruple when it came to sex. The rose-tinted glasses had been cruelly wrenched off when she was least able to cope and vulnerable, forced to see with her own eyes how sleazy her chosen partner was. Awash with disgust, she had called him a man whore and stalked away with her head held high, concealing her agonised hurt. And it had been *agonised*, she conceded painfully. Rio Benedetti had knocked her for six and unravelled her emotionally for months after that night.

It had been too sordid a story to share with Polly, who would have been even more shocked to the extent that her sister might have discussed Ellie's experience with Rashad, and Ellie had not been able to bear the prospect of her humiliation being more widely known. At least what had happened had happened more or less in private.

Someone rapped on her bedroom door and she opened it, expecting it to be the maid because she had said she was going out after breakfast and the room would be free. She didn't use the peephole and was sharply disconcerted when she realised that Rio had followed her upstairs to her room.

Fixing her attention doggedly on his red silk tie, she said curtly, 'I don't want to speak to you... Leave me alone—'

'No can do, *principessa*. If only this living and learning life were so simple,' Rio intoned mockingly.

'Don't call me that!' she snapped. 'And you're not coming in—'

A brown lean-fingered hand curved round the door in silent threat and he moved forward but Ellie stood her ground. She had faced drunks in A & E, dealt with drug addicts and violent people, and she wasn't about to be intimidated by Rio Benedetti.

'I don't think you want me to say what I have to say out here where I could be overheard,' Rio murmured sibilantly. 'It won't embarrass me—'

'*Nothing* embarrasses you!' Ellie snapped with very real loathing.

'It's about Beppe…Beppe Sorrentino,' Rio extended, watching her face like a hawk.

And Ellie surprised herself by stepping back to let him into the room because she absolutely *had* to know what he had to say on that subject. She knew he didn't know the mission she was on in Italy and that she wanted to try to establish her

father's identity. She was convinced that Rashad
was far too reserved and protective of his own
wife's privacy to have shared anything but the
sketchiest details about Ellie and Polly's background. But that Rio should even know Beppe's
name disturbed her.

'You can come in for five minutes...five minutes only,' Ellie negotiated thinly. 'And then I
want you to go away and forget you ever knew
me.'

Rio's beautiful mouth curled, his whole car-
riage screaming that he wasn't convinced by that
claim.

'And I warn you... If you smirk, I will slap
you again.'

CHAPTER TWO

'I DO NOT SMIRK,' Rio retorted very drily.

'Oh, yes, you do… You always look awfully pleased with yourself!' Ellie snapped back, her nerves all of a quiver and her brain no longer in control of her tongue because Rio in a confined space was too much for her.

It wasn't a large room. She had gone for cheap and cheerful in the accommodation stakes because she was planning to stay for an entire month in Italy and a classier room would have swallowed her budget within two weeks. But in a room already crowded with a double bed and a big wardrobe, Rio stole all the available space because he was very tall, at least six foot three and large from his broad shoulders to his lean hips and long, powerful legs. Her momentarily distracted gaze ran over the entirety of his sculpted physique, outlined as it was by a wickedly tailored suit that was sufficiently sophisticated to strike a formal note, but which also sensually delineated his muscular strength with fidelity. Colour flared in her pale face as she suddenly realised what she was doing and glanced away, her mouth running dry, her breathing disrupted and her thoughts overpowered by the stricken fear that he could somehow guess what she felt by the way she looked at him. Guess that she hated him but *still* thought he was gorgeous and incredibly tempting and incredibly bad for her like too much ice cream...

'Let's cut to the chase. What are you *doing* in Tuscany?' Rio demanded and it was a demand as only Rio could make it, every accented vowel laced with command and hostility.

'That's none of your business,' Ellie told him flatly.

'Beppe's my business... He's my godfather.' Lustrous dark eyes landed on her like laser beams, watching her face, keen to construe her expression.

Ellie froze in receipt of the very bad news he had just dropped on her from a height and in a defensive move she lowered her eyes. Rio actually *knew* Beppe Sorrentino and, even worse, had a familial relationship with the older man.

'You wrote to him looking for information about some woman he met well over twenty years ago,' he prompted doggedly, his dismissal of the likelihood of such a request clear in every word.

'Not some woman, my mother,' Ellie corrected, seeing no harm in confirming a truth he was already acquainted with. It was quite probable that Rio had already read her very carefully constructed letter to his godfather. Naturally she had mentioned nothing about boyfriends, pregnancies or putative fathers in it. She had been discreet, fearful of ruffling feathers and causing offence, but she did plan to question the older man to establish whether or not he knew anything about her paternity. It might be a long shot but it was the *only* shot she had. Beppe's friendly response to her letter had encouraged her and lightened her heart but the discovery that Rio Benedetti could be involved in any way in her very private quest for information infuriated her. Was she never to escape the shadow of that misguided night in Dharia?

'A mother whom you somehow know nothing about?' Rio pressed in a disbelieving tone.

'I was a newborn when my mother placed me in my grandmother's care. I never knew her,' Ellie admitted grudgingly, throwing him a look of hatred because she deeply resented being forced to tell him anything personal.

'Don't look at me like that when it's a lie,' Rio urged with staggering abruptness, fiery sparks illuminating his stunning eyes to smouldering gold.

The sudden apparent change of subject disconcerted Ellie. 'What's a lie?'

'You looking at me with dislike when you would really much prefer to rip my clothes off me!' Rio contended without an ounce of doubt in his dark deep drawl.

'Is that how you get women?' Ellie asked drily even while the betraying colour of mortification was creeping up her throat in a hot, seething tide. 'You tell *them* that they want you?'

'No, I only need to see you blush like a tomato to know I've hit pay dirt,' Rio countered with satisfaction. 'I don't do pretences, *principessa.*'

Even while betraying red climbed her face, the absolute curse of her fair colouring, Ellie stared back at him in genuine fascination. 'You honestly think I'm here for you and that my letter to your godfather is just some silly excuse to see you again? Oh, my word, Rio, how did you get through the door with an ego that big?'

'I hate the way you beat all around the bush instead of just coming to the point. It is a very *simple* point, after all,' Rio told her impatiently, wondering how the hell his dialogue with her had suddenly turned personal but somehow unable to stop it in its tracks.

'We're not having this conversation,' Ellie responded icily.

'You're not my teacher or my doctor, so you can drop the haughty chilling tone,' Rio advised, lounging back against the bedroom door, his sudden slumberous relaxation screaming sex and the kind of bad-boy attitude that set Ellie on fire with fury and curled her fingers into claws.

'We were talking about Beppe,' she reminded him in desperation.

'No. I was talking about us having angry sex—'

Ellie reddened again, her green eyes luminous with disbelief. 'You did *not* just say that to me—'

Rio laughed with unholy amusement. 'I did. Why wrap it up like a dirty secret? We may not like each other but, *per meraviglia*, with the chemistry we've got we would set the bed on fire—'

Ellie focussed on him because she refused to let her gaze drop, lest he take it as a coy invitation. But it *was* a mistake to meet those stunning dark golden eyes of his, a mistake to be close enough to note the luxuriant curling length of his black lashes and the hint of stubble accentuating the shape of his full-modelled mouth. Rio Benedetti made her think of sex. It was instinctual, utterly brazen and when she collided with his eyes it was as if he were operating a gravitational pull on her. Ellie's body turned so rigid that her muscles hurt but even that reality couldn't block the tide of physical awareness flooding her every skin cell. With deep bitter chagrin, she felt the pulse at the aching heart of her thighs and the swollen sensitivity of her breasts.

'Angry sex could be a lot of fun, *principessa*. It would loosen you up. You are very, *very* tense and I know exactly how to take care of that,' Rio purred, cool as ice water, his pride soothed by her dilated pupils and revealing flush. After all, if he had to tolerate being constantly aroused around her, why shouldn't she have to suffer the same? But in contrast to him why couldn't she be practical and honest about it? Did she still expect and demand the fake flowers-and-diamonds approach from the men in her life?

'That's enough.' Ellie lifted her chin and closed a hand into his sleeve to yank him off the door so that she could reach for the handle, but it was like trying to move a very large and heavy boulder and he didn't budge an inch.

'You really do enjoy getting physical with

me in other ways, don't you?' Rio derided huskily, looking down at her from his intimidating
height, wicked amusement dancing in his beautiful dark eyes. 'Is that a hint about your prefer-
ences? I'm not into bondage but I can definitely
picture you in one of those dominatrix outfits,
twirling a whip—'

And that was it for Ellie. He wouldn't move
from the door and he wouldn't shut up and frustration made her temper spontaneously combust
inside her and shoot up through her like a rocket.
'If you don't get out of here, I'm going to call the
police!' she screamed at him.

Rio flicked an imaginary speck of fluff from
the sleeve her tight grip had creased infinitesi-
mally. 'Fortunately the *polizia locale* are unlikely
to arrest a native for making a pass at a beautiful woman—'

'I don't care!' Ellie lashed back at him, all patience and restraint stripped from her. 'I hate
you...I want you out of my room...*now*!'

'When you tell me what you *really* want from

Beppe I'll leave,' Rio bargained softly. 'I want the truth.'

'It's private and it's none of your business and I won't allow you to bully me!' Ellie retorted angrily. 'Does your godfather even know that you're here tormenting me?'

Rio fell very still, reluctantly recognising that he was dealing with a quarry worthy of his mettle. Beppe was an old-fashioned gentleman and particularly protective of the female sex and he would be shocked by Rio's interference.

'I didn't think he did,' Ellie declared in the telling silence. 'The letter he sent me was kind and friendly. So back off, Rio, or I'll—'

'Or you'll what?' Rio growled in raw interruption. 'You think that you can threaten *me*?'

'Unlike you I'm not in the habit of threatening people,' Ellie countered, lifting her chin, her green eyes deeply troubled.

'Well, then let us reach an agreement here and now,' Rio suggested silkily. 'I could approach Beppe with the results of the investigative report I've had done on you and, if I did so, you would be turned away from the door tomorrow because there are enough dynamite allegations against you in that report to make him very wary.'

Ellie took an uncertain step backwards, hugely disconcerted by that accusation coming out of nowhere at her. 'I haven't done anything wrong, so I can't imagine what you're talking about—'

'Of course you're going to say that,' Rio parried, unimpressed. 'But the point is that serious allegations have been made against you and by more than one person.'

Ellie fell silent because, although she was innocent of any wrongdoing and had been cleared during an internal enquiry, a serious allegation *had* been lodged against her, which could have had a most negative impact on her career as a doctor. Fortunately for her, she was protected by National Health Service rules there to safeguard staff in such situations and the allegation had been withdrawn and the complaint dismissed. Tears stung the backs of her eyes because that same allegation had caused Ellie a great deal of stress and many sleepless nights before it had been settled and she had viewed her Italian holiday as a much-needed period of rest and recuperation. To have that unpleasant business, in which she had been truly blameless, flung in her teeth by Rio Benedetti was seriously offensive.

'Those allegations were dismissed a week before I flew out here,' she spelt out curtly, struggling to control the wobble in her voice. 'And what were you doing getting an investigative report done on me, for goodness' sake?'

'I will always protect Beppe from anyone who could take advantage of him and I don't trust you or the coincidence that brings you here,' Rio stated grimly, noting the sheen in her eyes, wondering if it was fake, deciding not to be impressed because tears in a woman's eyes were nothing new to his experience. Virtually every woman he had ever been with had done the crying thing at some stage and all it had ever done was chase him off faster.

'That's not my problem,' Ellie traded with an unapologetic little sniff that strangely enough impressed Rio much more than the hint of tears.

'And why would it even occur to you that I would *try* to take advantage of Beppe? Obviously you don't believe it but I'm not a dishonest person—'

At that claim, Rio quirked a sardonic ebony brow and thought about the diamond brooch she had somehow prevented her uncle from inheriting. 'Aren't you? Even though you can't even bring yourself to admit that you want me—'

'You know why—because nothing is going to happen between us,' Ellie told him piously, superiority ringing in every syllable. 'Why acknowledge it?'

And there it was again, that intonation that made Rio want to do or say something totally outrageous. It shot him straight back to his misspent youth when he had been regularly carpeted for his sins in Sister Teresa's school office. There was something so incredibly frustrating about Ellie's blanket ban on normal sexual behaviour, he reasoned angrily. He could not understand why a woman with so much pent-up passion should repeatedly strive to ignore the sizzle in the air between them. As if attraction was a weakness? Or a risk she wasn't prepared to take?

His own convoluted and uncharacteristic thoughts on that score exasperated him as much as they had in Dharia. The evening of her sister's wedding had been a washout but that hadn't been his fault, had it been? Ellie had been totally unreasonable and unjust when she'd blamed him for that episode. He had been honest with her, as well, *too* honest, and where had that got him? A slap on the face and a shedload of insults. They would never have worked anyway, he told himself impatiently, not with a woman seemingly hardwired to be touchy, angry and super judgemental.

'*Non c'è problema...* Don't worry about it,' Rio advised drily as he swung round and pulled open the door. 'But when you fall, I'll still be the one to catch you.'

'I won't be falling. Can I hope this is the last I'll be seeing of you?' Ellie dared as he strode out into the corridor and involuntarily she too stepped over the threshold.

'You have nothing to fear from me unless you distress or damage Beppe in some way,' Rio warned, his voice roughening at the mere thought of any harm coming to the older man. 'I don't know why you're being so secretive anyway. Beppe will eventually tell me what this was all about.'

Pretending sublime indifference to that prospect, Ellie shrugged a slight shoulder. 'Why would I care?' she said breezily, keen to discourage his suspicions that she was hiding anything of a serious nature.

But she *did* care. Rio could see it in her unusually expressive and anxious gaze. He realised that there was definitely a secret of some sort that connected Ellie to his godfather and that disturbed him because for the life of him he could not imagine any likely connection. Beppe, for one thing, had never travelled outside Italy and was very much a home bird. It occurred to him for the first time that perhaps he should have investigated the mother rather than the daughter, but unwisely he had overlooked that option because Ellie inspired greater curiosity.

'You *do* care,' Rio traded softly, moving slightly closer.

In a skittish move, Ellie backed up against the door of her room. 'I'm a very private person,' she stated in a stubborn refusal to admit even the smallest weakness, because Rio was 100 per cent shark and she knew the blood in the water would be hers if she gave so much as an inch.

'Not always,' Rio disagreed, suddenly right there in front of her, eating her alive with his black-lashed smouldering eyes. A lean brown forefinger trailed gently down the side of her hot face.

She felt every tiny second of that fleeting caress like a brand burning right through to the centre of her body. She wasn't used to being touched, she told herself bracingly, should've been dating more, should've been less of a perfectionist, should've been less sensible. His eyes above hers flamed gold and she recalled a moment exactly like that on the dance floor in Dharia, and in a

clumsy movement she tried to peel herself off
the door into her room and safety but it was too
late, way too late when Rio's beautifully shaped
mouth came crashing down on hers.

And that kiss was something between a car
crash and a shot of adrenalin in her veins. Her
body came alive with a great whoosh of physical response and her hands flew up into his
hair, touching, shaping, *clutching* the springy
strands. And she wanted him as a dehydrated
woman wanted water, as if he were the only
thing that stood between her and death. That
ferocious, screaming shout of need that instantly
controlled her absolutely terrified her. The spear
of his tongue in her mouth electrified her beyond
all thought and the flick against the roof of her
mouth was pure licking temptation by a maestro
of sensation. He knew how to kiss, he knew how
to do all the stuff she didn't and that drew her
helplessly, that and the merciless craving making
her heart beat too fast, making her body tremble
and her legs weak.

'*Inferno*, Ellie...' Rio growled against her

swollen mouth, rocking his hips ever so slightly against her.

And she could feel him through their clothing, long and hard and urgent with the same need that had already overwhelmed her and she shuddered, fighting for control against all the odds and without words, knowing that no, whatever happened, she just couldn't do this with him.

But Rio, womaniser that he was, kissed her again and again; being Rio, he had upped his game. Slow and tormenting had become rawly passionate and demanding and every skin cell in her body lit up in neon as if she had met her perfect match. The pulsing damp heat between her thighs was coalescing into a generalised burning ache that tortured and tempted and screamed. The sound of a metal bucket scraping across tiles was almost deafening and Rio sprang back from her at the same instant that Ellie literally forced her hands down to his shoulders to push him away.

And for once, Rio didn't have anything super smart to say, she noted with only the smallest amount of satisfaction because she had nothing to boast about either. Rio dealt her a scorchingly angry glance and swung away.

'I'll be in touch,' he said grittily.

'Not if I see you coming first,' Ellie quipped weakly, ducking back into her room under the curious appraisal of the cleaner and closing the door on legs that felt as limp as cotton wool. But *no*, she was not going to do that thing she usually did when she did something wrong. She wasn't going to dwell on it and go over it endlessly. She had made a mistake and it was already behind her and that was all the brooding Rio Benedetti deserved. No more self-loathing, no more regret, she told herself squarely. He was like a cup of poison that tasted sweet, created only to tempt and destroy. Paranoiac…much, she asked herself then.

CHAPTER THREE

THAT MORNING, ELLIE explored the village, bought a small gift for a colleague and walked in the glorious sunshine through the *piazza* to the café to take a seat. She was beginning to enjoy herself, starting to recognise that beating herself up about Rio was counterproductive because it kept him in the forefront of her mind. One kiss… What was a kiss? *Nothing!* Well, unless it made your knees go weak and threw your brain into la-la land—then it was a threat.

While she sipped her coffee, crossly policing her thoughts, she watched an opulent cream sports car park. The driver, who had a little dog with him, hailed several locals seated outside the café and his attention lingered on Ellie before he strode across the *piazza* to enter the shop there. The dog, however, a bouncy little Yorkshire terrier, hurtled straight across to Ellie and bounced up against her legs, craving attention.

The dog's owner shouted what sounded like, 'Bambi!' in an exasperated voice but the dog wouldn't budge from Ellie's feet and, with an audible groan and a wave that promised his return, the young man went on ahead into the shop.

'You're not the most obedient dog,' Ellie scolded softly a few minutes later as pleading little round eyes appealed to her from knee height. 'No, you can't get up on my lap. I'm not a doggy person—'

'You could've fooled me,' the owner remarked from beside her and she glanced up and laughed.

'Well, I suspect your dog's not very fussy,' she teased.

'Bambi belongs to my mother and I'm looking after the dog all week.' He rolled his eyes in speaking suffering. 'She hasn't been trained and prefers women.'

'But that's not her fault,' Ellie pointed out, scratching a blissed-out Bambi behind one flyaway ear.

'I'm Bruno Nigrelli.' He extended a friendly hand. 'Join me for a glass of wine—'

'A little early,' Ellie began before she recalled that she was on holiday and not on duty. 'No, that's a good idea,' she told him with a sudden smile. Loosen up, she told herself irritably.

Bruno stayed with her for about half an hour, making easy comfortable conversation, and it was so relaxing after the emotional angst of dealing with Rio, Ellie acknowledged ruefully. Bruno was a contracts lawyer based in Florence and he was currently staying at his mother's home to look after it while she was away. When he asked her to dine with him the following evening, Ellie agreed. Polly's voice was ringing loudly in her ears. 'Attractive man—tick. Employed—tick. Good manners—tick. Stop looking for what's wrong with every man you meet!' Polly had told her that the reason she rarely dated was that she was far too fussy. But Ellie didn't think that was fair because when it came to men, Polly had proved equally hard to impress.

The following morning, Ellie drove her little hire car to Beppe's impressive *palazzo*. The huge gates stood wide in readiness for her arrival. She drove slowly through the elaborate gravelled gardens that fronted the big house and parked, climbing out, smoothing damp palms down over the casual white skirt she had teamed with a navy-and-white tee and canvas espadrilles. She walked up the shallow steps to the front door and a youthful manservant in a very correct black jacket opened it before she could even reach for the bell.

'Ellie Dixon for Mr Sorrentino,' she said helpfully.

'Yes,' he said gruffly in English. 'He waits for you.'

Ellie was a mass of nerves and trying not to show it. Could Beppe *be* her...? No, she refused to think about that because it wasn't very likely when Beppe had been married at the time. The more likely scenario would be Beppe telling her that he hadn't known her mother well enough to give her any useful information as to who her father might be.

'Miss Dixon...' A small man near her own height greeted her at the door of a book-lined room with a warm smile. 'Come in and sit down. Adriano will bring us morning coffee.'

With a soft sound of pleasure she sat down in the chair overlooking the beautiful garden. 'This is such a comfortable room,' she told him cheerfully. 'All these books and bits and pieces are fascinating and when you throw the view in, as well—'

'I'm a lifelong collector and passionate gardener,' Beppe admitted as he sat down opposite her.

'Thank you for being willing to see me like this,' Ellie said a little awkwardly. 'I can only hope that I'm not about to say anything that may make you regret it—'

'I don't take offence easily,' Beppe reassured her. 'But I confess that I'm very curious about your mother. What happened to her after she left Italy?'

'I didn't even know for sure that she *had* been in Italy, although it was a fairly obvious assumption,' Ellie admitted, opting for complete honesty as she dug into her bag and extracted the emerald ring. 'My mother left me this ring...'

Beppe paled, his easy smile slipping for an instant. He scooped up the ring at the same time as the door opened and Adriano brought in a tray. He spoke to the young man with a couple of hand signals. 'Adriano's deaf,' he muttered absently, his attention still fixedly focussed on the emerald.

'He's a great lip-reader,' Ellie remarked.

'He's had a lot of training over the years. Once he's acquired the necessary experience working here, he hopes to find a more exciting position abroad,' Beppe told her and he leant forward to deposit the ring back on the table beside her cup. '*I* gave your mother this ring. It once belonged to my mother,' he added heavily.

'Okay.' Taken aback by that admission, Ellie nodded acceptance. 'So you knew her well?'

'Better than I should have done in the circumstances,' Beppe confided in a weighted undertone of discomfiture. 'Annabel spent that summer working for an English family who had a holiday home not far from here. My brother, Vincenzo, met her first and they got engaged before I even met her. I think you would call it a whirlwind romance because they had only known each other for a few weeks.'

Ellie sighed, thinking of what she had learned about her mother from her sister Polly. 'What year was that?'

Beppe told her and the timing dovetailed in Ellie's mind. Her older sister would only have been a toddler when Annabel came to work in Italy.

'How do I describe Annabel to you...her daughter?' Beppe sighed. 'She was full of life and tremendous fun to be with but she was a little impulsive when it came to love.'

'Yes,' Ellie agreed, wondering what was coming next.

'I was married to a wife who was disabled. That is *not* an excuse. There can be no excuse for what happened,' Beppe continued with unconcealed regret. 'I learned that I was not the man I believed I was. I fell head over heels in love with your mother and it was the same for her. I was thirty-five then, hardly an impressionable boy, and I fully believed that I loved my wife. Amalia was a wonderful wife. It was not an unhappy marriage yet I broke her heart and my brother's. But mercifully, *generously* my brother did not choose to publicly accuse me of what I had done and my wife was not humiliated. Together, Amalia and I concentrated on restoring our marriage, locked away that secret affair and moved on.'

'I honestly don't know what I can say to what you've just told me because I know none of the people involved,' Ellie said carefully. 'But I am sorry to hear that other people were injured by my mother's actions.'

'Annabel injured herself most of all. She could've had a good life with my brother but she gave him up because she met me,' Beppe admitted with remorse. 'Vincenzo was still estranged from me when he died. It was a horrible mess for all of us—'

'I'm very sorry,' Ellie breathed, feeling inadequate in the face of such honesty and a very personal story, which she had never expected to hear told.

'The last time I saw your mother she was very angry with me,' Beppe confessed unhappily. 'I had told her from the outset of our affair that I would not leave my wife but she refused to accept that. My love for my wife was a different kind of love but no less real to me. Although I was an unfaithful husband, Amalia forgave me and we stayed together and we were blessed by many more happy years before she passed away...'

'My goodness...I genuinely didn't come here to cause you distress, but I can see that I've done nothing but rake up disastrous memories!' Ellie exclaimed guiltily, seeing the tears that shone in Beppe's dark eyes. 'Unfortunately, I came here with a very different angle, Beppe. I'm trying to find out who my father is—'

'In Italy?' he cut in, his surprise unconcealed. 'Surely you are far too young to believe you were conceived *here*? When were you born?'

And she told him and his face became very

sombre. 'I believed you were several years younger, but it is certainly a possibility that I could be the man you seek. *Dio mio*, that could explain why your mother told me that I would live to regret not leaving my wife for her.'

Ellie fell silent, disturbed by the harsh nature of what she was learning about the mother she had never known.

'*We* will have to look into this more. With tests? That is how it is done, is it not?'

'Are you willing to do that?'

'*Certamente...* Of course,' Beppe responded. 'Now perhaps we should discuss something less challenging while we consider what we have both learned.'

Ellie's hand shook a little as she lifted her cup because she was marvelling at his calm manner.

Beppe chuckled. 'I must be on my very best behaviour now in case you turn out to be a relative.'

And Ellie's hopes soared, that he was the man, that he would turn out to be her father and that a lifetime of frustrating speculation would be ended. They parted an hour later with Beppe promising to contact a doctor he was friendly with, who would advise them discreetly on their quest. Tears rolled down Ellie's cheeks as she drove back to her hotel. She was in a daze and she was praying that Beppe would be the man she sought because she had really, *really* liked him and it would be beyond wonderful to discover a father she could actually connect with as a person.

Rio, however, had a very different experience when he joined his godfather for lunch. After what transpired there, bitter anger consumed him and when he left he headed straight to Ellie's hotel, determined to confront her. Learning that she had gone for a walk to a local landmark, he set off to follow her in his car.

Ellie paused halfway up the very steep hill and wiped the perspiration from her brow, registering that in such sultry heat, she had tackled a challenge too great for her fitness level. Hearing the sound of an approaching vehicle, she stepped back onto the verge. She was disconcerted to see Rio at the wheel of a very racy scarlet sports car.

He braked and leant across to open the passenger door. 'Get in!' he told her uninvitingly.

'No, thanks,' Ellie responded. Her day had been demanding enough without adding him into it.

Without a word, Rio shot her an intimidating glance from molten gold eyes and sprang out of the car, stalked round the bonnet, and before she could even guess his intention he had scooped her off her startled feet and dropped her into the passenger seat, slamming the door after her.

'What the heck do you think you're playing at?' Ellie yelled at him in disbelief as she struggled to open the door to get out again and failed because he had already engaged the child lock to prevent her from doing exactly that.

Rio shot back behind the wheel, his lean, darkly handsome face granite hard. 'We have to talk—'

'No, we don't. I have *nothing* to say to you!' Ellie proclaimed vehemently. 'Let me out of this car—'

'Put your seat belt on!' Rio growled at her as if she hadn't spoken.

'No, I won't. I refuse to go anywhere with you!' Ellie yelled back at him.

Rio leant across her to wrench the seat belt round her and she was so taken aback by the second act enforced against her wishes that she studied him in shock. 'This is kidnapping and assault,' she informed him furiously. 'I will go to the police and make an official complaint about you!'

'Go ahead!' Rio bit out rawly.

'You are out of control,' Ellie informed him. 'You're not thinking about what you're doing!'

'*Sì*... If I'd thought about it, I would have come armed with a gag!' Rio slung at her wrathfully.

'Much good that would do you. I'm a judo black belt,' Ellie countered. 'Had I known you were planning to kidnap me, I would have defended myself to stop you grabbing me.'

'Don't kid yourself,' Rio practically spat at her as he raked the car on up the hill she had been struggling to climb. 'If you were assaulted, you would be far too busy assessing the pros and cons of acting aggressively to take action quickly enough to defend yourself!'

And Ellie was stunned by that eerily accurate reading of her character. Rio was the single exception to her abhorrence of violence in all its forms and even when it came to him she didn't want to actually *hurt* him, just hold him at bay or make him go away. 'Where are you taking me?'

'Somewhere we can talk in peace,' he grated.

Ellie skimmed an infuriated glance at his set profile, noting the classic slope of his nose, the definition lent by his perfect cheekbones, the outrageous sweep of his black lashes. 'You're driving too fast—'

'I am within the speed limit.'

Ellie flung her head back with a sigh of frustration, her wild mane of hair blowing in the wind. She would look like a rag doll with corkscrew curls by the time she got out of the car but what did that matter? The breeze against her overheated skin was wonderfully cooling. Kidnapping and assault? Rio had a temper worse than her own and that was a revelation that had a surprisingly cooling effect on Ellie's own temper. She had learned young that she had to learn to control and contain the ferocity of her feelings. Rio, evidently, had not. The oddest sense of compassion flooded her because she had not a doubt that he would be very embarrassed when he looked back and fully thought through what he had done to her.

Rio, however, was in a rage to surpass all rages and he was well aware of it. Beppe's distress had provoked a visceral reaction in him that he could not deny or fight. He *loved* that man, would have done anything for him! That he had failed to shield Beppe from whatever nasty business Ellie had somehow involved him in slashed Rio's proud protective spirit to the bone. He was going to get the truth out of Ellie if it killed him. *Inferno...* This mysterious nonsense everybody was refusing to discuss had to end right now because his patience was at an end!

Rio turned the car off the road down a long track. Dense clusters of ancient oak trees prevented Ellie from seeing more than a few yards ahead and when the car rounded the final bend she had no inkling that they were heading for a house until she saw it right there in front of her. It was a breathtaking *palazzo*, with a remarkable resemblance to an elaborate dolls' house, and it fitted into the landscape where it had clearly held its commanding position for centuries. It was built on a hill and undoubtedly had views that stretched for miles. She unclasped her seat belt and climbed out with a look of exasperated tolerance in Rio's direction once the child lock was finally disengaged.

'You can apologise now,' Ellie said.

'Apologise?' Rio practically roared at her in disbelief. 'Beppe was in *tears* over lunch! I haven't seen him in such a state since his wife died. What did you do to him?'

Ellie froze beside the car, her fine-boned features locking tight, her pallor noticeable. Clearly she had upset Beppe Sorrentino and yet she had never wanted to do that. Had she ever truly considered what her quest to discover her father would do to the man involved? No, she hadn't, she conceded guiltily. In fact, she had believed that it would be *safe* to approach Beppe because he was a childless widower who seemed to have no close relatives. Of course, she hadn't known about Rio's connection to the older man then and, seeing the intensity of Rio's fury, she instantly recognised that he was attached to Beppe and it hit her hard. Rio might not be a blood relative but the way he was reacting he might as well have been.

'I didn't do anything to Beppe. I simply gave him some information he wasn't expecting to hear,' Ellie countered uncomfortably, because what on earth was she supposed to say to Rio?

If Beppe hadn't told his godson the truth, it was certainly not her place to do so. And she quite understood the older man's reasoning. He had had an affair while he was married, an affair that more than twenty years on he still obviously regretted. He was ashamed of his affair with her mother and Ellie had to respect that reality. It hurt to appreciate that, even if tests were done and Beppe did prove to be her father, he might well want the existence of an illegitimate daughter to remain a secret. She couldn't fairly complain about that, couldn't possibly resent it because Beppe had the right to guard his privacy and make his own choices. That he had agreed to DNA testing was more than enough, she told herself doggedly, scolding herself for the fantasy of having a *real* father, which she had rather naively begun to entertain. Really, how likely was it that Beppe would seek an ongoing relationship with her now that she was an adult and fully independent?

'Ellie!' Rio raked back impatiently at her as he stalked back from the front door he had unlocked. She had once watched a tiger pace a cage in the same way and it was distinctly unnerving. For the first time it dawned on her that so volatile a personality should have frightened her and she was even more surprised to acknowledge that, not only was she unafraid, but also ridiculously attracted by Rio's sheer sizzling intensity. Even so, she wished that like a difficult piece of technology Rio came with a useful book of in-

structions because she didn't know how she was supposed to calm him down when she wasn't in a position to give him the explanation he so plainly wanted.

'The raised voice is getting really *old*,' Ellie told him drily instead.

Dark colour scored his razor-sharp cheekbones. 'Come inside—'

'Said the kidnapper to his victim,' Ellie added.

Rio swore in a flood of Italian.

'Yes, I give as good as I get,' Ellie pointed out, moving out of the sunshine into the shadow of the building because calling Rio's bluff was one thing, but baking alive while doing it would be foolish.

'I brought you to my home because I desired privacy in which to speak to you,' Rio framed with obvious difficulty in being that polite.

Ellie pondered her options, which were few. She had neither her phone nor any money on her person. Rio had stranded her in the Tuscan countryside. 'I'll come inside but there will be no more shouting and you will not put your hands on me again,' she warned him.

'I can't promise that I won't shout because I am very angry with you,' Rio admitted in a low-pitched growl as he watched her move towards him, her skirt fluttering above her slender knees, making him very aware of the long shapely legs beneath. His gaze filtered involuntarily upward, lingering on the soft fullness of her pink lips, and shifted with a jerk as she moved, the luscious sway of her full breasts below her top making his mouth run dry. 'And I wouldn't promise to keep my hands off you because I'm not sure I could ever deliver on that one, *principessa*.'

That honest response and possibly the reuse of that mocking label worked for Ellie and released a little of her nervous tension. In fact, she went pink while inwardly admitting that she wasn't that much better at keeping her hands off him, regardless of whether she was slapping him or kissing him. Rio awakened very strong reactions inside her. The usual barriers that she employed to keep a careful distance from people were shockingly absent with Rio Benedetti and that awareness rattled her nerves.

Ellie followed Rio into a cool, tiled hallway that was strikingly contemporary and into a vast reception room furnished with pale leather sofas and several dramatic modern paintings. The gorgeous house might be ancient but the cool interior decor and modern furnishings were in stark contrast.

Rio spun round to face her again, a dark shadow of stubble accentuating his beautifully shaped mouth and the raw tension etched in the hard line of his lips. And she found herself wondering for the first time if he was ever gentle or tender, traits that seemed far removed from his aggressive, competitive nature. And did it even matter, another voice mocked, when he looked the way he did? That mocking inner voice shocked her because it steamrollered over everything she believed she knew about herself, for since when had she been impressed by appearances? Yet when she looked at Rio, everything sane and sensible vanished from her brain as if it had been wiped.

And then there was only room for glorying in his tempestuous male magnificence, room to marvel at the precise arrangement of his lean, darkly charismatic features and the stunning clarity of his smouldering golden eyes. She sucked in a startled breath to fill her deprived lungs.

'All I'm asking you to do is come clean with me,' Rio murmured lightly, as though what he was asking should be easy for her to do. 'Tell me what's going on...'

Ellie's slim figure tensed. 'It's not that simple, Rio.'

An ebony brow quirked in disagreement. 'It is a very simple matter that you are making difficult out of sheer stubbornness.'

'No, it is a private matter between Beppe and me,' she countered. 'Ask *him* to explain things.'

His intent gaze narrowed. 'You must know that I will not do anything more to upset him.'

'And I will not break his confidence without his permission, so we're at an impasse—'

'Have some wine,' Rio suggested wryly, strolling over to the drinks cabinet and giving her a choice.

'Rosé, but it won't loosen my tongue,' she warned him doggedly, but the extreme tension in her knees holding her stiff gave way a tad, reminding her that her meeting with Beppe and the walk had exhausted her.

'Help me out here…I am *trying* to be civilised,' Rio informed her.

'There was nothing civilised about the way you stuffed me in your car,' Ellie reminded him drily as she settled down on a sofa.

'*Per l'amor di Dio*, I never said I was perfect, *principessa*.'

'Why do you call me that?' she demanded abruptly as he settled a moisture-beaded wine glass into her hand, momentarily standing so close to her that the scent of him assailed her: hot, musky male laced with a hint of spicy cologne. A very faint shiver ricocheted through her.

Rio grinned and it was an unexpectedly boyish grin of keen amusement. 'Because the way you walk with your little superior nose in the air gives you that look. You remind me of the rich girls I used to watch when I was a penniless teenager. Oh, they looked at me, but they wouldn't have dirtied their lily-white hands by *touching* me.'

'I was never a rich girl,' Ellie parried uncomfortably, studying him with grass-green eyes that were luminous in the filtered sunshine and alive with curiosity. 'I grew up in my grandmother's working-class home and there were no airs or graces there.'

'*Cio nonostante...* Nonetheless you ooze that rich-girl quality of disdain,' Rio told her with assurance. 'And it sets my teeth on edge—'

'Everything about me sets your teeth on edge,' Ellie pointed out wryly while she wondered about his background, because she was surprised that he had ever been penniless and on the outside looking in at the more prosperous. '*We* annoy each other.'

'Beppe,' he reminded her darkly. 'Talk.'

In a sudden movement, Ellie stood up again because he was making her feel trapped. She understood exactly where he was coming from but she couldn't answer his questions. His godfather *could* have enlightened him and had chosen not to. Beppe's silence spoke for him. Clearly he had no desire to admit to Rio that he had had an extramarital affair or that that liaison could have led to the conception of a child.

'I don't back down, Ellie,' Rio murmured from close by and every skin cell in her body jumped at the knock-on effect of that deep accented drawl of his, goosebumps rising on her bare arms. 'I won't let you go until you fill in the blanks—'

'Well, then, you're going to be stuck with me!' Ellie exclaimed in growing frustration. 'Because I'm not going to talk—'

Rio removed the glass from her fingers and set it aside. 'Maybe talking's a total waste of time for us, *principessa*.'

'And what's that supposed to mean?' Ellie demanded thinly even though she had a very good idea.

Rio scored a light forefinger across her compressed lower lip. 'You're pushing it defying me. I don't have your patience—'

Ellie threw her head back, corkscrew curls tumbling across her pale brow, green eyes sharp with frustration and defensiveness. 'Don't touch me!' she warned him curtly.

'No, not a shred of patience,' Rio asserted with hypnotic quietness, reaching for her with scorching dark golden eyes of sensual threat.

CHAPTER FOUR

'I CAME INTO this house with you because I trusted you,' Ellie declared starkly, twisting away.

'No, you don't. You don't trust me,' Rio assured her with grim amusement. 'You most probably came into the house because you don't like arguments in public and you are nervous of how far I would go to win.'

'Well, doesn't that just say it all about you?' Ellie quipped.

'You know nothing about me yet you still judge,' Rio condemned.

Ellie stilled, disconcerted by that criticism, and Rio took advantage of her momentary abstraction. His arm curved to her spine and he yanked her close, bringing her up against the hard, unyielding strength of his lean, powerful body, and her hormones leapt as though he had electrified her. His mouth nibbled along the plump fullness of her lower lip and all of a sudden she couldn't breathe for anticipation. Her lips parted for him, letting his tongue plunge deep, and an aching sweetness that drowned every thought rose from the very heart of her. Something in the furthest reaches of her brain was saying no, no, *no*, but all the rest of her was in open rebellion.

It was the kiss to end all kisses, fit to eradicate any previous kiss because no man had ever made Ellie's head swim with a kiss before. She felt dizzy and delirious, utterly unlike herself, adrenalin charging through her veins and lighting her up as though she had crossed the finishing line of a race. Her fingers delved freely into his springy black hair, sheer delight at the freedom to touch him consuming her.

Overwhelmed by her response, Rio tensed, wondering when it would end and abandoning any plan to stage a slow seduction scene. He had never wanted any woman as he wanted Ellie Dixon. Need was already flaming through him like a burning torch. One hand at the shallow indentation of her spine, he ground against her, so hard, so ready, so overpoweringly hungry for the damp release of her body that he trembled. It didn't make sense to him. Yes, she was a challenge, but no woman had ever come between Rio and his wits. He was in control, he was always in control, but this one time, he *wasn't*. Shouldn't that worry him? He shelved the question, too much lost in the moment to waste time considering the drawbacks and inconsistencies. He brought Ellie down on the sofa and kissed her with unashamed passion.

'What are we…doing?' Ellie mumbled through swollen lips as Rio whipped off her top, exposing the heavy-duty white lace confection she wore to confine the breasts that she considered to be too large. It was a stupid question and she knew it and the sight of her own almost bare flesh unnerved her and filled her with discomfiture.

'*Sta' zitto*... Shut up!' Rio urged, burying his face between those utterly magnificent breasts while wrestling with a bra that had more restrictive hooks than a corset. If she talked, she would talk herself out of it, he thought in consternation, and he looked down into her beautiful eyes, emerald as the most precious of jewels, and told her to close them.

'You are incredible' was wrenched from him, breaking his self-imposed silence as he studied the lush creamy swell of her glorious breasts. An awed fingertip brushed a large pink nipple already pouting for his attention. He wanted to carry her up to his bedroom, spread her out and enjoy her as she should be enjoyed but he didn't want to break the spell.

Instead he bent his dark head and succumbed to the considerable allure of her breasts. He whisked his tongue over a rigid bud the colour of a tea rose and teased the tortured peak, loving the way she shifted under him, instantly responsive to his every caress.

Ellie had fallen so deep that she was drowning in the world of sensation she had always denied herself. The hunger in her for *more* was unbearable. Her breasts throbbed, sending messages to the lush damp place between her shifting thighs.

Her hips lifted in frustration. She wanted Rio everywhere at once. She wanted the impossible. She also wanted his clothes off with a strength of craving that shook her because it was not as though she was a stranger to the male anatomy. In frustration, she hauled at the shoulders of his jacket and he reared back from her with a sudden surprised laugh and peeled it off to pitch it on the floor.

'And the shirt,' Ellie instructed him shakily, scarcely believing what she was doing, what she was participating in, and unable to dwell on it lest her caution yank her back from the edge. And she wanted Rio, she wanted him so much that she was weak from the wanting and the never-ending wondering and longing that had dogged her since the day they had first met.

A couple of shirt buttons came loose of their stitching as Rio ripped off the shirt with an almost joyful air of abandonment. He was all lean muscle sheathed in sleek bronzed skin from his wide shoulders to his narrow waist and she stared helplessly entranced and surprised at her visceral reaction to his masculinity. As the shirt dropped, he smiled at her in a way he had never smiled before and that slanting, teasing grin was purebred enticement on his darkly beautiful face. Indeed that smile had so much appeal that she sat up and hauled him down towards her to claim his devastating mouth for herself again.

He lay on his side, kissing her breathless and she revelled in every kiss and the brush of his skilled fingers over her wildly sensitised breasts. He pushed up her skirt and traced the edges of her panties, teasing, tormenting, making her agonisingly aware of just how desperate she was to be touched. A finger slid beneath the lace and stroked her swollen folds. She was wet, so wet she was embarrassed by her body and its screaming eagerness. A fingertip circled her and suddenly there was no room for embarrassment, no room for anything but her own gasping, jerking response. He took away that final barrier and explored her.

He shimmied down the sofa and used his mouth on that tender place between her thighs and if lying still had been a challenge before it soon became an impossible challenge for Ellie. Her fingers clawed into his luxuriant black hair, her body dancing and twisting to the powerful drumbeat of desire. The sensations he evoked were excruciatingly intense and only heightened the tormenting ache of need building deep in her pelvis. Heat gathered and mounted uncontrollably at the heart of her and then, taking her entirely by surprise, exploded outwards in a violent climax of sweet, shattering pleasure.

'*Madre di Dio*...I can't wait to be inside you, *bella mia*,' Rio said huskily, rearranging her and sliding fluidly between her parted thighs. 'I am so hungry for you.'

Do I want this? Ellie asked herself and she knew she didn't need to ask that question because when she looked up into Rio's gorgeous dark eyes she was ready to agree to do anything he wanted to do. It was as though she were in a dream without a past or a future or even a present. She felt as though there was nothing but that moment and she liked it that way.

Rio tilted her back and drove into her with a single powerful thrust. And Ellie twisted her head to one side and bit her lip because it hurt, it hurt much more than she had expected, and that burning sting of pain wrenched a muffled little moan of discomfort from between her gritted teeth.

'Something wrong?' Rio rasped, lifting his tousled dark head. '*Dio mio*, you are so tight you feel like a virgin!'

'I *am*!' Ellie gasped before she could think better of making that admission.

Rio had already sunk as deep as he could get into her tiny body and he froze in shock to gaze down at her. 'A virgin?' he echoed in ringing disbelief. 'How can you be a virgin?'

Ellie wrinkled her nose. 'Oh, just get it over with, for goodness' sake,' she told him in desperation.

Stunned by that irreverent urging, Rio took several seconds to absorb what had happened. She was a virgin? How was that possible? And why hadn't he noticed anything different about her? He shifted position, withdrawing and then slowly gliding back. *Get it over with?* What was he? An ordeal to be endured?

The friction of his movement created a little hum of pulsing sensation low in Ellie's body. She shut her eyes tight, refusing to think, indeed terrified to allow herself to think about what she had just done, what she had just allowed him to do. And while she was battening down her mental hatches, Rio was putting every atom of skill he possessed into rescuing the situation. But he was hugely aroused and working alone because Ellie lay there under him like a little felled tree.

He pushed her knees up and ground down into her, delving deeper, setting an insistent rhythm that she couldn't ignore. Her hips lifted but much against her will because she was set on simply tolerating him. A frenzied heat began to build and she fought it off as though it were a forest fire. Her hips rose involuntarily and he slammed down into her, sending a startling pulse of pleasure through her. Her heart thumped like crazy, the ability to breathe stolen from her as he picked up speed and force and dominated her. Wild excitement surged and gripped her but much against her will. Her hands bit into his shoulders and then slid caressingly down his muscular back as this time she sensed the peak she was reaching towards.

A chain reaction of convulsions claimed her and she cried out as the ripples of ecstasy spread in a blinding moment of release that consumed her. Rio shuddered and held her tight and bit out something raw and rough in Italian, his powerful body surging into hers. Within seconds, however, she was free again, watching in a daze as Rio sprang off the sofa to fix his trousers and reach for his shirt.

'You were a virgin?' Rio repeated incredulously, because innocence and Ellie were a combination that refused to compute in his brain.

Wincing, Ellie sat up and pushed down her skirt. Her panties were lying on the tiles but she had no intention of trying to reclaim them in front of him. She was shell-shocked and shattered by what had taken place. She couldn't believe she had had sex with Rio. Just then in the aftermath it looked like the worst decision ever after a lifetime of vigilant caution.

'A virgin?' Rio prompted again as if a virgin were as improbable as a glimpse of a unicorn. 'So, why give it up to me?'

'Maybe I wanted to lose it with someone who would put me off further experimentation,' Ellie suggested with honeyed derision. 'Stop acting as if you've been grievously assaulted by a virgin, Rio. I can't be the first you've been with—'

'You *are*!' Rio contradicted accusingly, taken aback by her gutsy attitude.

Ellie stood up, very discreetly retrieved her underwear and, quite deliberately ignoring him, went off in search of a cloakroom. It actually hurt to walk, she acknowledged in shock. She ached as though they had had sex for hours. The experience felt less like an introduction and more like a lesson. Be careful of what you wish for, she told herself unhappily. He had leapt off that sofa as though he had been electrocuted. Innocence was clearly a hanging offence in Rio's book.

Another much more worrying fact was screaming along the edge of Rio's ragged nerves while he paced the hall, waiting impatiently for Ellie to reappear. He had never met a woman like Ellie and he was very certain that he never wanted to meet another. She drove him crazy. She made him do and say things he never did or said with anyone else. She screwed with his brain, unleashed his temper and sent him racing off the edge of sanity. She had the seductive powers of a temptress and yet how could that be when she had self-evidently had no sexual experience whatsoever? He was terrific in bed and he knew that but she had behaved as though he were useless. So, why did he want her to stay the night? Simply to rescue his ego? And what about Beppe? *And what about the lack of a condom?* He groaned out loud in frustration and raked his fingers through his cropped black curls. Rio felt *raw*.

Only innate courage persuaded Ellie out of the sanctuary of the cloakroom because in reality she wanted to curl up and die somewhere well out of Rio's sight and reach. She didn't want to see him again; she didn't want to have to speak to him again either. She simply wanted to forget what had happened and continue her holiday.

'Please drive me back to my hotel,' she said woodenly, refusing to look directly at him.

'Are you on the pill? Or any other form of contraception?' Rio asked her with startling abruptness.

Ellie almost flinched. She had spent a year taking contraceptive pills after her sobering experience with Rio at her sister's wedding. She had feared meeting that level of temptation again and as a result had taken sensible precautions to protect herself in the future. Sadly, however, she had suffered side effects from the medication and had stopped taking the pills.

'No. I'm not.' Ellie shook her head slowly and walked back into the reception room to sit down again, because she felt literally weak with shock and anxiety. 'How could we both be so stupid?'

'There are still...options,' Rio selected in a grim undertone.

Ellie's head reared up, fiery corkscrew curls

tumbling back from her white forehead, accentuating her bright green eyes. 'Don't you dare suggest options to me! I'm a doctor, sworn to protect life,' she shot back at him.

'I didn't say that *that* was what I wanted. *Accidenti!* We are not reckless teenagers but we behaved as though we were,' Rio intoned in open exasperation. 'When we get together it is as though we are cursed. Let us hope there are no consequences...'

CHAPTER FIVE

ELLIE BREATHED IN deeply and slowly released her breath in the hope of chasing away the brain fog afflicting her ability to think. She was struggling to perform little mental calculations around her menstrual cycle, very quickly realising that their timing had been little short of catastrophic. She had chosen the worst possible moment to abandon her usual caution, she recognised in steadily deepening dismay.

What if Rio made her pregnant? The consequences of unprotected sex were not something she wanted to contemplate, particularly when she had a very poor relationship with the potential father. She suppressed a fearful shudder and told herself to be strong. Whatever happened, it would happen and she couldn't change that. In the meantime it would be best to go on as though nothing had changed.

'Please take me back to my hotel or call me a taxi or something,' Ellie muttered in desperation.

'You still haven't told me what you've done to Beppe—'

'I haven't done anything to him!' Ellie proclaimed in a sudden fury roused by the stabbing of her conscience. After all, if Beppe Sorrentino was troubled, it *was* her fault because she had told him something that had upset him. She had been selfish and thoughtless, dwelling only on her right to know who her father was without ever considering the cost that that information might inflict on anyone else. Even worse, Rio was Beppe's godson and Beppe had no idea that Ellie had already met Rio and was currently involved with the younger man. But *was* she involved with him?

Ellie grimaced at the concept because that word, *involved*, lent a gravitas to their entanglement that it didn't deserve. They had engaged in a foolish and irresponsible sexual encounter, nothing more. They weren't in a relationship, nor were they likely to be. And how did she feel about that reality? And the answer was that that reality saddened and wounded her heart and her pride. With Rio, she was slowly and painfully learning that she was more vulnerable than she had ever appreciated. She had made a mistake with him two years earlier and almost unbelievably had made an even bigger mistake this time around. Sex might be a field that Rio played in but Ellie didn't play at anything she did. She didn't do casual either.

'Ellie...' Rio breathed impatiently.

Ellie rose from her seat to move back out to the hall. 'I can't discuss Beppe with you. I'm sorry but that's how it is—'

'What are you hiding from me?' Glittering dark eyes full of suspicion locked to the pale triangle of Ellie's face.

Ellie lifted her chin. 'People have secrets, Rio. Secrets they don't want to share. Dragging them out into the light of day isn't always the right thing to do,' she reasoned uneasily.

'Beppe has no secrets… He's not that kind of man,' Rio argued with sublime assurance. 'So, if you're not judging, you're preaching. Are you so perfect?'

'No, I know I'm far from perfect and I wasn't preaching. I was just speaking my thoughts out loud. I'm a little confused right now,' Ellie admitted tightly, her eyes suddenly stinging while she wondered if her entire trip to Italy had been an outsize blunder. Maybe she should have left the past buried, maybe she should've tried harder to suppress her curiosity. All she knew was that she felt very guilty at the knowledge that Beppe had been distressed by her visit. He had dealt with her kindly but perhaps she hadn't deserved that kindness.

'I'll take you back to the hotel,' Rio murmured without any expression at all. He had reached the conclusion that it would take a hacksaw to extract anything from Ellie that she did not want to share. What secrets was she concealing? What he had read in that investigative report? Or was there more?

'Yes, thank you. I have a da—' Ellie bit off the word before it could reach the tip of her tongue but she saw Rio's dark gaze switch fast to her face and she felt her cheeks burn.

'You have a date?' Rio pressed in growling disbelief, staring at her as she stood there in the comparative dimness of the hall, a glowing beauty with a sexily tousled mane of vibrant coppery curls, translucent skin and a mouth that would've tempted a saint. And he had never been a saint. Even less was he known as a possessive lover, because he didn't allow himself to become attached: once bitten, twice shy. So why did the very thought of Ellie becoming intimate with another man infuriate him? Disconcerted by that rush of anger, he tamped it down hard and gritted his teeth.

'A guy I met in the village invited me out to dinner tonight,' Ellie confided in a rush.

'His name?' Rio demanded.

'Bruno Nigrelli.'

Rio's nostrils flared. 'I think he did some work for Beppe once. Lawyer?'

Ellie nodded uncomfortably.

Rio gritted his teeth even harder in the smouldering silence. Was she expecting him to object? Even waiting for him to do so? Wasn't that how women sucked a man in, by assigning strings and conditions and making him want and demand more?

'I'm not much in the mood for dinner now, but I don't like letting people down—'

Rio's dark eyes flared golden as the sunset. 'Then cancel him and spend the night here with me instead.'

Ellie froze in bewilderment, green eyes flying over his lean, darkly handsome features. 'Spend the night?' she repeated shakily.

'It would make more sense—'

Ellie dropped her gaze defensively. 'Nothing about us makes sense—'

'We make perfect sense. You decided I was a *bastardo* two years ago and even if I saved the world you wouldn't budge an inch from that conviction,' Rio derided.

'I think a lot of women would think the same

after that night at the wedding, but let's not get into that,' Ellie counselled heavily as she yanked open the hefty front door. 'We have enough differences without raking up the past. I can't stay, Rio—'

'Ellie... When will you know?'

Ellie dropped her head as she settled into the passenger seat of his sports car. 'In ten days to two weeks,' she framed jaggedly. 'I'll do a test as soon as I can.'

In the sunlight, Rio stood very still. What would he do if Ellie conceived his child? He recalled his own sordid origins with an inner shudder of recoil, knowing in that instant that there would be no sacrifice too great were it to mean that his child could look back with pride and contentment on his or her early years. Only when Beppe and Amalia took an interest in him had Rio learned what it was to have self-respect. Being cleverer than everyone around him had only attracted the bullies. Being prettier as a boy had also drawn the abusers. His lean, strong face was stamped by the grim lines and hollows of bitter recollection and experience. As an adult, Rio Benedetti might be as rich as the fabled Croesus but he had never forgotten his humble beginnings in that dumpster.

Ellie glanced up to see what was preventing Rio from joining her in the car and ended up staring, because it was a revelation to see that Rio, all lean, mean and magnificent six-foot-plus of him, could look haunted and almost vulnerable. She scolded herself for that imaginative flight as soon as he started up the car but his rebuke about her tendency to judge was still nagging at the back of her mind. Sometimes she was kind of black-and-white about situations, she acknowledged uneasily, but just as she had learned all her life to follow rules she *had* learned to compromise and understand what motivated people to do the things they did, as well. She supposed she *was* still holding the events of two years earlier against Rio because his colourful sex life had shocked her. As someone who had never pushed against conventional boundaries, possibly she *was* a little too conservative for a passionate free spirit like Rio.

Rio pulled the car to a halt in the hotel car park. He shot Ellie a glance, noting the fineness of her delicate bone structure and how clearly it showed beneath her pale skin. She was exhausted and he could see it and he compressed his mouth on the urge to make another comment about Beppe. He refused to think about the dinner date she had. He refused to admit that the idea annoyed him. After all, he wasn't possessive and he wasn't jealous. He didn't *ever* get attached to a woman— well, at least he hadn't in almost ten years.

And when Rio *had* got attached—to Franca—it had been a disaster, he recalled grimly. Treachery laced with infidelity and a woman's greed. Rio had learned the hard way that loving could be a one-way ticket to hell.

No, he definitely wasn't jealous. He already knew that Ellie was a gold-digger, he reminded himself resolutely. He would only care about Ellie Dixon's future if she became pregnant with his child. In the short term his *sole* interest in her lay in uncovering her mysterious connection to Beppe.

Rio sprang out of the car and strode round to open the passenger door. Disconcerted by that unexpected attention, Ellie climbed out and as she looked up warily into his glitteringly beautiful dark golden eyes, the sunlight hot on her skin, her conscience screamed like a fire alarm. She had been downright nasty about the sex even though he had been considerate and concerned and, bearing in mind that he had given her two climaxes, she had been unjust. Her skin flushed beet red.

'*Che cosa...* What?' Rio pressed in the strained silence.

'I shouldn't have said what I said back at your house,' Ellie gabbled before she could lose her nerve. 'It was a train wreck... Us, I mean, and me being...well, you know what. But you were good, I mean—'

Rio wanted to laugh but he fought the urge because she was so embarrassed, so utterly different from him in her attitude to sex. 'Okay...'

'I'm sorry,' Ellie said curtly. 'I was…I was upset.'

And with that apology she spun on her heel and walked into the hotel. Her head had a natural tilt, her hips a shapely sway, the skirt dancing above her long slender legs and, that fast, Rio was hard as a rock again, his hands clenching into fists by his sides. She drove him crazy, he reminded himself unnecessarily. But he had had her now and that should be that, game over. Hit it and quit it, he repeated to himself. He didn't *still* want her. Of course he didn't, so walk away, a little voice in his brain instructed.

Rio swung back into his car. The sound of Ellie moaning as he kissed her engulfed him, the surprised look of ecstasy on her face when she came, the exquisite feel of her soft, satiny skin. He swore vehemently, emptied his mind and dug out his phone. He needed a woman, *any* woman just as long as she wasn't Ellie.

In a daze, Ellie went for a shower. She still ached. There would be no forgetting what she had done.

And the incredulous way Rio had looked at her in the car park would stay with her until the day she died. Her face burned afresh. She should have kept quiet, she shouldn't have said anything, should have left that short-lived intimacy and all memory of it back in his house in the hills where it belonged. A mistaken moment and not an important one in her scheme of things. Only sex. Although it would not be *only* sex if she fell pregnant, she conceded wretchedly, and refused to think about that angle on the grounds that it was stupid to worry before she knew she actually had something to worry about.

Although for the first time ever, Ellie desperately wanted to confide in someone and she thought about phoning Polly. She didn't think Polly would tell her husband, Rashad, about *that*. But how did she know for sure? She covered her face with wet hands, all the stress of the past forty-eight hours piling up on her along with every doubt and insecurity she possessed. She still didn't know how she had ended up having sex with Rio, but she knew she had wanted it to happen as much as he had. Being unable to put the blame on him stung, as well. He hadn't sweet-talked her, filled her up with booze or seduced her—*my goodness, anything but*, she conceded ruefully.

Beppe called her on her mobile and asked her to meet him at a doctor's surgery on the outskirts of Florence the next day. She refused the lift he offered her and assured him that she had satellite navigation and was happy to drive herself there. He invited her to dine at his home in the evening and she agreed, keen to take the opportunity to get to know him a little better, regardless of how Rio might feel about it. Should she tell Beppe that she knew Rio? Or would it be wiser to remain tactfully silent? She brooded about that while she got dressed to dine with Bruno.

It was a long evening. Bruno might have ticked all the basic boxes in the tally of what made a man attractive but he bored on about his work ambitions while asking little about Ellie. He kissed her on the cheek outside her hotel. He invited her out again and she made a polite excuse and she didn't linger, speeding indoors, keen to get to bed.

Opening the door of her hotel room, she drew back with a sound of consternation when she saw the light burning beside her bed and the male reclining there. 'How on earth did you get in here?' she demanded.

Rio uncoiled fluidly off the bed and stretched with lazy assurance, not one whit perturbed by her attitude. 'It wasn't difficult. The staff know we're...close,' he selected with precision and the angry flush on her cheeks bloomed hotter still with chagrin. 'I also own a large stake in the hotel.'

'We are *not* close!' Ellie contradicted, tossing her bag down on the chair in the corner.

Rio shrugged a broad shoulder, gracefully and silently evasive. He was as effortlessly beautiful as a dark angel sent to tempt even with his black hair tousled, his jawline shadowed and his tie missing. Her heartbeat had picked up speed. Her tiredness had taken a mysterious step back and she was already breathing as if she had run up a hill. And there was the craziest melting sensation in that place where she still ached from his sheer sexual energy. Yet she didn't want *that* again, did she? It was a badly timed thought to have in Rio's presence because her entire body quickened as if she had punched a button to switch it on to supersensitivity. Her nipples stung and her thighs pressed together as if to silence the squirming readiness low in her pelvis.

'Are you planning to tell me what you're doing here?' Ellie enquired stiffly, tamping down all those disobedient thoughts and responses.

'I wanted to be sure you came back alone,' Rio told her.

'And how is that your business?'

'You were with me today,' Rio murmured.

Ellie tilted her chin, emerald eyes gleaming like chips of ice. 'Doesn't mean you own me.'

Rio shrugged again. 'I'd still have beaten the hell out of him had you brought him upstairs.'

Ellie's lips parted and then closed again because there really wasn't much she could say to that. 'You do a lot of that sort of thing?' she prompted a split second later, honest curiosity gripping her.

'Get physical? Once it was a regular activity.' Dark eyes spilling a glittering gleam of gold from below lush curling black lashes, Rio strode past her to the door. 'I had to, to protect myself. I grew up in a tough environment.'

'You're leaving?' Ellie framed in disconcertion and then could have bitten her tongue out because she was making it sound as though she wanted him to stay. And she didn't.

'*Si...*' Rio treated her to a slow burning appraisal. 'Somehow I doubt that you'd be up for anything else tonight, *principessa*.'

Fury splintered through Ellie. Leave it to Rio to tell it as it is. He would stay for sex but not to chat or share a drink or supper or anything more civilised. The claustrophobic silence of the room enclosed her, increasing her nervous tension. The tip of her tongue stole out to moisten her dry lower lip.

'I *love* your mouth,' Rio husked soft and low,

his attention locking to the sultry fullness of her pink lips.

Gooseflesh pebbled Ellie's arms and a wicked little quiver snaked down her taut spinal cord. She was so aware of him that her very skin prickled and tingled with it. For an insane moment she imagined pushing him backwards down on the bed and teaching him that he didn't know everything about her. And then she blinked, sane Ellie swimming back to the fore, and she spun and opened the door for him so that he would leave more quickly.

'Sometimes you crack me up, *bella mia*,' Rio confided with unholy amusement, recognising her defensiveness in that almost desperate pulling open of the door to hasten his departure. 'When you're thinking about me in bed tonight, will you be kissing me or thumping me?'

Ellie breathed in so deep she almost spontaneously combusted while she watched Rio clatter down the stairs without an ounce of discomfiture in his bearing. She had never met anyone quite like Rio Benedetti before and that was probably why he knocked her for six every time she saw him, she told herself soothingly. He was bad, he was brash, he was incredibly sexy and insolent and he had the kind of charismatic confidence that burned like a solar flare. She was too polite and inhibited to deal with him as he *should* be dealt with. Her hands clenched into fists.

He embarrassed her too. The staff had seen her going out with Bruno Nigrelli and now knew she had returned to find Rio waiting in her bedroom. Ought she to complain about that invasion? Or, having already been seen in Rio's company and kissing him, perhaps it was wiser to ignore the situation lest she end up even more embarrassed. Had Rio made her look slutty? Or like a femme fatale? She went to bed on that thought, deciding that Rio's pursuit, if she could label it with that word, made her look like a much more exciting woman than she actually was. But she still wanted to kill him for being so careless of appearances, so arrogant and incomprehensible.

Why would he have beaten up Bruno had she brought the other man back to her room? Presumably that had been a joke, although she had not seen the humour in it. She could not credit that Rio could be jealous or staking some sort of male claim to her. He wasn't the type. And instead of finding the sleep she badly needed the riddle of his complex personality ensured that she couldn't stop her brain running on and actually relax enough to drift off.

The following morning she met up with Beppe outside a smart suburban surgery near Florence. The older man looked perfectly calm and collected and there was no sign of strain or distress in either his expression or his friendly, easy manner. Had Rio exaggerated? Overreacted? They went inside the surgery and swabs were taken. Beppe passed over a tiny gold locket, which he quietly admitted contained a lock of his brother's hair. Ellie flushed and made no comment. After all, her mother, Annabel, had named both brothers as her daughter's possible father, and to do so, she had presumably been uncertain as to which had fathered her child.

'We will know within twenty-four hours,' Beppe assured her with quiet satisfaction. 'And now that I have you here in my beloved Firenze, I will play tourist with you and show you the sights as they should be seen.'

Relieved by his mood and the welcome offer of his company, Ellie relaxed and over a cup of coffee and a pastry in a sun-drenched square found herself admitting that she knew Rio and had first met him at her sister's wedding.

The older man did not hide his astonishment. 'He should've told me that—'

'To be honest,' Ellie added hurriedly, 'Rio and I didn't get on very well, so it wasn't an acquaintance either of us was likely to pursue.'

Beppe sighed. 'You surprise me. Women are drawn to my godson. Obviously you've seen him since your arrival—'

'He called in at the hotel on my first day. I didn't tell him anything,' Ellie assured him, her cheeks colouring when she was forced to think of what else she had done with Rio since that day, but it was a major relief for her to admit simply that she knew Rio.

'Rio put me on a pedestal a very long time ago,' Beppe confided wryly. 'If you and I discover that we are related by blood, it will be a huge shock for him and that is why I have told him nothing as yet.'

'Were you friends with his parents? I know he's your godson.'

'No, my wife and I never knew his parents,' Beppe admitted dismissively and changed the subject to ask her to choose where she would like to go first with him.

Beppe took her to see Michelangelo's sculptures in the Galleria dell'Academia before showing her his favourite paintings in the Uffizi. Her frank admission that she knew nothing whatsoever about art did her no disservice in his eyes and when she liked something he asked her *why* she liked it, evidently set on forming her taste. He also told her a little about his own family background. The *palazzo* had been in his family for several generations and the Sorrentino prosperity had originally been built on the production of internationally acclaimed wines. His younger brother, Vincenzo, had once managed the vineyards. Beppe had always been academic and had worked as a university professor before his wife's ill health had forced him to take a step back from his career. From that point on, he had become more involved in his wife's charitable endeavours, which had been very much focussed on the needs of disabled and disadvantaged children.

'What time is dinner this evening?' Ellie asked when Beppe had finally returned her to her car. She noted that he was out of breath and perspiring and she scolded herself for letting him do so much on a hot day when he was clearly by his girth and indoor habits not usually a physically active man.

'Nine o'clock. And it will be formal,' Beppe warned her. 'But don't worry about that if you have no formal wear with you. Everyone will understand that you are on holiday.'

Ellie smiled at that recollection as she returned to her hotel. Thanks to Polly's holiday shop, Ellie had a dream of a dress hanging in the wardrobe. In fact, uninterested though she had always been in fashion, it was the sort of dress that brought stars to her eyes because it was wonderfully feminine and flowing. Fashioned of peach lace, it was a daring colour for a redhead, but remarkably flattering against her pale skin and bright hair. She showered and paid more heed than usual to the minimal make-up she wore while wondering if Rio would be at the dinner. Would he be annoyed that she had gone ahead and told his godfather that they already knew each other? Staying silent on that score had become impossible for her because Beppe was so very straightforward and plain-spoken and she did not want to risk losing his good opinion by keeping secrets from him.

The gravel in front of Beppe's home was a sea of luxury-model cars, which disconcerted Ellie because evidently the dinner party was a much bigger, fancier event than she had assumed it would be. Her fear that she would prove to be overdressed receded as soon as she was shown into a crowded salon filled with clusters of very elegant laughing and chattering guests. Beppe hurried straight over to welcome her and tucked her hand over his arm protectively as he took her to join the group he was with. Within a few minutes, Ellie had relaxed.

And then the door opened again and she glanced across the room to see the new arrivals and saw Rio entering with a tall willowy blonde clinging to his arm. Her heart sank and she couldn't stop it from doing that. Her pleasant smile lurched and her tummy flipped and all of a sudden she felt ridiculously sick and shaky. What the heck was the matter with her? She was not in a relationship with Rio, was she? Why should it bother her that he was already showing off another woman? After all, she had known from the outset that he was a notorious womaniser with few moral scruples.

Rio was taken aback by Ellie's presence because Beppe hadn't mentioned that his visitor would be attending. Nor did it help that Ellie looked stupendous in an apricot dress that smoothly shaped her lush curves at breast and hip while highlighting her porcelain-pale skin and the sheer vibrancy of her coppery tumbling mane of hair. His physical response was swift and urgent, the swelling at his groin an unwelcome reminder that 'hit it and quit it' hadn't worked for him where she was concerned. Above her breast, she had fastened a diamond brooch in the shape of a star and it was the only jewellery she wore. So, she *did* have the diamond brooch her uncle had accused her of stealing, Rio recognised in sudden disgust, the brooch she had denied all knowledge of after her grandmother's death. For Rio, it was a timely reminder of the kind of woman he was dealing with in Ellie Dixon. At heart she had to be a greedy, gold-digging liar who had learned how to put on a good show as a caring, compassionate doctor.

Rio strode straight up to Beppe and introduced his gorgeous companion, who seemed unable to take her eyes off Ellie's dress. The blonde's name was Carmela and she was unquestionably beautiful and very different in style from Ellie. She was taller, thinner, blue-eyed and possessed enviably straight, long silky blond hair. Her dress was much more revealing than Ellie's but then she had a perfect body to reveal. A long slender leg showed through the side slit in the dress while the plunging neckline showed a great deal of her improbably large, high breasts. Gorgeous but kind of slutty, Ellie decided, discomfited by the speed with which that shrewish opinion came to her mind.

'Of course, Ellie needs no introduction to you, Rio,' his godfather, Beppe, pointed out smoothly as an opening salvo. 'Since you first met at her sister's wedding.'

Rio was transfixed by that bombshell reminder coming at him out of nowhere and unadulterated rage roared through his big powerful frame as his attention shot to Ellie, who evaded his gaze while slowly turning as red as a tomato, her guilt writ large in her face. Ellie had chosen to come clean with Beppe and had dropped him in it without conscience, Rio registered grimly. A power play? Or was it a warning? What else might she choose to tell his godfather about him? Shot through with anger and frustration at his inability to respond with the truth, Rio was incapable of even forcing a smile.

'We didn't hit it off,' Ellie said abruptly. 'That's why he didn't mention it.'

Shot from rage to wonderment at that apparent intervention on his behalf, Rio dealt Ellie a suspicious look from glittering dark-as-jet eyes semiveiled by his lush lashes and shrugged. 'First impressions are rarely reliable,' he quipped as he turned away to address someone else who had spoken to him.

Ellie was appalled that something she had revealed had caused tension between Rio and Beppe. Her trip to Italy and her search for her father were definitely beginning to feel like a minefield she was trying to pick her way across.

As Rio moved to grasp a glass from a tray and pass it to her, Carmela hissed, 'That redhead's wearing a Lavroff!'

Rio shot the fashion model on his arm a blank appraisal.

'That dress was the star of the Lavroff show I walked for in the spring.'

A designer gown, surely a little rich for a junior doctor's salary? Although perhaps not too expensive for a doctor whose dying patient had left her everything she possessed, Rio reflected sombrely. It was starting to occur to him that he had underestimated Ellie and how much trouble she was capable of causing. He could see at a glance that she already had Beppe wrapped round her little finger. In fact, her hand was resting comfortably on the older man's arm. Rio dragged in a sudden breath, his lean, darkly handsome features tensing into tough lines of restraint. Was *that* what he had to fear?

Ironically that risk hadn't even crossed his mind because Beppe lived a celibate life and had never been known to seek out female companionship. But Beppe had been acquainted with Ellie's mother, and if Ellie's mother had been even half as beautiful as her daughter, she would hardly have been forgettable. Back then, however, Beppe had been safely married and now he was not and he was making no attempt to hide his delight in Ellie's company. Rio stationed himself where he could watch his godfather and he was sharply disconcerted by the level of familiarity he could already see developing between the pair. Ellie whispered something in Beppe's ear and he chuckled and patted her hand fondly. He moved her on with him to another group of guests, giving her no opportunity to stray.

At his elbow, Carmela was still whinging on enviously about the Lavroff gown. Rio wasn't interested. He often paid for the designer clothes his lovers wore but he took no interest in the names or the cost, writing the expenses off as the cost of maintaining a reasonable sex life. His entire focus remained on Ellie. He listened to her making intelligent conversation, heard her laugh several times and learned that she had toured the Uffizi gallery with Beppe. *Inferno,* she certainly didn't need to be taught how to best please a much older, lonely man with a lifelong love of art. But she would soon learn her mistake if she persisted on her current ambitious trajectory. Rio would destroy her before he would allow her to hurt Beppe Sorrentino.

And what if she's pregnant? Rio backed away a step as Carmela tried to get closer to him. He studied Ellie as they were seated at the dining table and strove to imagine that shapely body swollen with his child. The idea unnerved him but it also excited him in a peculiar way, which only had the effect of unnerving him even more.

Ellie barely touched the food on her plate. She eavesdropped on Carmela's airheaded views on suntans as affected by climate change. She noticed that Rio didn't listen to a word his companion said and appeared to be tuning her out like an irritating noise. She watched him, as well, catching the downward slant of his beautifully shaped mouth, the tension in his exquisite bone structure that hardened his exotic cheekbones and placed hollows beneath them. He was furious with her, she *knew* he was. Rio had a temper like a flamethrower and he was boiling like a cauldron of oil.

But Ellie was angry too. Only the day before he had been with her and last night he had been waiting for her in her hotel room. And now he was with a beautiful blonde model, who operated off one very talkative brain cell. Why was she hurt? Why the hell was she hurting over his rejection of her as a woman? Time after time over the years Ellie had learned that men didn't really want career-driven, independent women. She wasn't feminine enough, she wasn't *soft* enough, she could deal with a spider just fine but a mouse sent her screaming. She was stubborn and contrary and choosy and he didn't fit the bill for her either, so why was she agonising? Why would she want a gorgeous, arrogant, shameless man whore in her life anyway? She was far too sensible and strait-laced for a male of his ilk. Sheer lust had put her in his arms and she had got what she deserved, she told herself repressively.

Beppe took her and several other guests to admire his latest painting acquisition in the hall. Rio and Carmela joined them. Carmela wondered out loud if the seventeenth-century subject of the portrait was wearing hair extensions. Ellie whispered a polite, 'Excuse me…' in Beppe's ear as he guided the group into his library to show them something else and she walked down the corridor to the cloakroom instead. Freshening up, she grimaced at her anxious reflection in the mirror. Why was it that when Rio was around he dominated everything? Including her thoughts?

When she emerged, Rio was standing waiting for her, his lean, dark face stormy and tense. 'I want a word,' he told her grimly.

'But I *don't*,' Ellie told him as he snapped a hand round her wrist and pulled her outdoors onto the cool, formal *loggia* with pillars that ran along that side of the house.

'You're such a bully, Rio!' Ellie objected, rubbing her wrist the instant he released it as though he had bruised her.

Rio backed her up against the stone wall behind her by the simple expedient of moving forward, shutting out any view of the gardens and forcing her to tip her head back to look up at him. 'What did you tell Beppe about us?' he demanded in a raw undertone.

'Very little. That we met at the wedding and

that you called on me at the hotel the day I arrived,' Ellie proffered. 'I didn't tell him what you said or threatened or anything of that nature. I simply wanted to clear the air. Pretending we were strangers...I mean, why would I mislead Beppe like that? I've got nothing to hide—'

'Not according to the report I had done on you,' Rio reminded her darkly.

Ellie bridled at that reference, fully convinced that any close and proper check on her background would reveal that she was innocent of any wrongdoing. 'I didn't intend to cause friction between you and Beppe. I didn't think of that angle,' she admitted guiltily. 'But I'm sorry that I embarrassed you like that—'

'Are you really?' Rio lifted a sardonic ebony brow, staring down at her, noting the mere hint at her neckline of the pale valley between her full breasts and entranced by the new discovery that showing so little could actually be sexier than showing a lot. As he tensed, inescapably recalling his own response to those luscious curves the day before, he whipped his gaze up to her face in the hope of lowering his temperature. 'I think you dropped me in it deliberately to cause trouble,' he contended.

'But then you would think that because you always think the worst of me,' Ellie shot back at him in exasperation. 'Exactly what is your problem, Rio?'

Rio ran his fingertip along the succulent curve of her lower lip and watched a tiny pulse flicker fast at the base of her elegant white throat. 'You're my only problem, *principessa*,' he told her huskily. 'We had our moment and that was supposed to be it—'

'It *is* it!' Ellie seethed, furious that he was cornering her when he had brought another woman to dinner.

'Not for me,' Rio confided, letting a coppery corkscrew curl coil round his finger like a vine, his stunning dark golden eyes hot and hungrily gripping hers by sheer force of will. 'I'm not done yet—'

'But I *am*,' Ellie spelled out thinly. 'You're ruining my holiday—'

'When we're done, I'll *tell* you,' Rio asserted, bending down to nip at her full lower lip with the edge of his teeth.

A violent shiver ran down through her taut body, that tiny sting of pain somehow setting off a chain reaction of electrified awareness and sensitivity. He lowered his head and he took her mouth with a raw sexual demand that momentarily stole Ellie's wits. She fell back against the wall, knees weak, melting heat surging in her pelvis.

'*Rio!*' a voice interposed curtly, and both of them froze.

Rio lifted his dark head and stepped back to study his godfather, keen to interpret his expression. Beppe looked angry and protective. Ellie straightened, her face flushing as mortification consumed her.

'Carmela's looking for you,' Beppe murmured flatly. 'I suggest that you take her home. I would also suggest that you stay away from Ellie.'

Rio released his breath in an audible hiss. 'Although I'm always ready to listen to suggestions,

Beppe,' he conceded, 'I've always forged my own path.'

With a nod of acknowledgement to Ellie and the older man, Rio strode back indoors, not one whit perturbed by the scene Beppe had interrupted. Or, at least, if he was bothered, he wasn't showing it, Ellie acknowledged.

'I have no right to interfere,' Beppe said uncomfortably to Ellie. 'I love Rio like a son but I also know him. He had some unfortunate experiences with women in his youth and I would advise you to keep your distance. He plays with women. He doesn't take them seriously. He would hurt you and I would hate to see that happen. Furthermore, if you prove to be either my niece or even my daughter, you will often meet Rio and that—'

'Could get very awkward,' Ellie filled in ruefully for herself. 'It's all right, Beppe. I kind of worked out that stuff about Rio anyway, so don't worry about me. I'm a big girl and I can look after myself.'

Rio and Carmela were nowhere to be seen

when they rejoined the rest of the guests. Ellie stayed quite late but insisted on returning to her hotel when Beppe offered her the use of a guest room. She drove back in a contemplative state of mind and wondered if she would find Rio in her room again. Not this time however.

Soberly she lay in bed, wondering about the results of the DNA test. Would she prove to be half-Sorrentino? Or was she in for a shock on that score? It was perfectly possible, after all, that some time after Beppe's rejection her mother had spent a night with some other man. Well, at least she would soon know one way or another, even if she didn't actually manage to identify her father, she told herself soothingly.

But how would Rio react if she was a Sorrentino? Ironically she didn't want to upset him but nor was she willing to apologise for an act of fate. She was already wondering what Beppe's mention of Rio's 'unfortunate youthful experiences' with women had entailed. But then surely no intelligent male could be so innately distrustful and cynical about her sex without cause?

And what did it matter? She relived the teasing sting of his teeth on her lip and a forbidden little quiver snaked through her. With a groan she rolled over and pressed her offending mouth into the pillow. Rio was as potent as poison and equally toxic and Beppe was right, she *needed* to keep her distance. To do anything else would be to court disaster because Rio had no off switch, no respect for boundaries…and probably even less respect for her, she conceded unhappily.

CHAPTER SIX

BEPPE CALLED ELLIE bright and early and asked her to come to his home. Ellie surmised that he had bad news and she took her time over her breakfast in the hotel courtyard, trying not to stress over what could not be changed. Beppe had been wonderfully approachable and kind and helpful and she wanted to thank him for that. He could've denied any knowledge of her late mother but instead he had told her the unvarnished truth, even though doing so had raked up guilty memories and regrets.

Ellie drove over to the *palazzo* and Adriano showed her out to the shaded *loggia*, quickly reappearing with a tray of coffee and biscuits. Beppe appeared then, rather flushed in appearance and with eyes that were a little shiny.

He studied her and he then smiled widely, a

smile brimming with happiness and appreciation. 'Ellie,' he began emotively as he handed her a sheet of paper to study. 'You *are* my daughter and I cannot begin to describe how much that discovery means to me.'

Lively with excitement, Beppe could hardly be persuaded to drink his coffee as he ignored her medical training to explain rather unnecessarily the 99.99 recurring percentage of accuracy established by the successful DNA test. 'I would've been delighted to discover that you were my niece but to discover a daughter, a first child after all these years, is an unimaginable joy!'

Ellie reached across the small circular table and grasped his hand to squeeze it. 'Thank you for saying that.'

'It comes from the centre of my heart,' Beppe told her warmly. 'Amalia give birth to a stillborn son just weeks before she suffered her stroke. We were devastated. I don't believe, though, that I could have told her about you were she still alive. It would have hurt her too much and my affair had already caused her enormous grief.'

'How do you think Rio will take this news?' Ellie asked, dry-mouthed.

Beppe emitted a heavy sigh. 'He will be here for lunch and I will tell him then. He will be happy that I am happy but very disappointed to hear that I once betrayed Amalia. If only we had adopted him as I wished, he would have been more certain of his place in the family.'

Ellie sat forward, brow furrowed, her curiosity engaged. 'You wanted to *adopt* Rio?'

'*Sì*. I will respect his privacy by not giving you details but he had neither parents nor a home and I wanted to take him in, but Amalia refused to set another child in what she always viewed as our stillborn son's place,' he confided heavily. 'There were also elements of Rio's background which disturbed her and she could not be persuaded to change her mind. He never knew that I wanted to adopt him though. Our contribution to his life became less direct as he grew up. We advised him, ensured he got a good education and supported him when he needed us but we could have protected him a great deal more had we adopted him and brought him up here.'

'That's unfortunate but Rio has still done very well for himself, hasn't he?'

'If you measure success by prosperity, his wealth reached stratospheric proportions after he won the oil contracts in Dharia. He is very much a self-made man,' Beppe declared with pride. 'But he is also a man damaged by a traumatic childhood and a tough adolescence. I should've done more for him.'

'By the sound of it, you did the best you could in the circumstances,' Ellie remarked soothingly, troubled more than she liked by the reference to Rio's traumatic childhood and troubled adolescence. Yes, she could imagine how such experiences would have hardened him and what a difference a loving, supportive home background could have made. After all, she knew that she too was marked by the lack of love in her childhood. Her grandmother hadn't wanted to raise her daughter's two illegitimate children and had only done so because Annabel had paid her handsomely to take on that responsibility. When that flow of money had stopped, presumably because Annabel had suffered bankruptcy and ill health, her grandmother had complained bitterly about how much of a burden her granddaughters were. Polly's affection had provided the only love Ellie had experienced during those years.

'I think I'll go back to the hotel now,' Ellie announced, hardening herself to Beppe's look of disappointment. 'Rio will be arriving soon and we both need some time to think. This is a lot to take on board and so much more than I ever expected to learn.'

'I hope you will pack and come here to stay with me for what remains of your holiday,' Beppe admitted. 'And perhaps someday you will feel comfortable enough to call me *Papà.*'

Ellie's eyes prickled with tears as she left. She felt ridiculously emotional and when Beppe gave her a small, almost daring hug on the doorstep it almost made the pent-up tears spill down her cheeks. He was willing to be her father and she was in a daze of shock and happiness. It bothered her to appreciate that Rio was unlikely to celebrate the same news. Rio didn't like her and didn't trust her and the revelation that she was his precious godfather's daughter would hit him hard. Would it hurt him that she had the blood tie with Beppe that he had been denied? She flinched from the thought, marvelling at how oversensitive she was to any thought of Rio being hurt.

It was so ridiculous, she thought ruefully. Big, tough, angry, hostile Rio would not be so easily hurt. Why was she even considering how he would feel about her parentage? What business was it of his? After all, the scene had been set before she was even born by Beppe's affair with her unhappy mother. By the sound of it that extramarital affair had caused tremendous unhappiness for all the parties involved, but surely after so many years Beppe could begin to forgive himself and both of them could now concentrate on forming a relationship? That conviction at the forefront of her mind, Ellie packed her case and then walked down to the village to kill some time and allow Beppe to speak to Rio in peace.

* * *

Rio departed from Beppe's home reeling from what his godfather had dropped on him. An adulterous affair and a daughter? No, he had certainly not seen that possibility on the horizon and it changed everything, his own position most of all. Ellie had played a blinder of a game by concealing her true motivation for being in Italy right to the very end, Rio acknowledged bitterly. In fact, she had trussed him up like a chicken ready for the roasting pot. Beppe had openly voiced his concern that Rio nourished dishonourable intentions towards his newfound daughter. Beppe had no idea that Rio had already gone much further than that and if he found out it would destroy his relationship with Rio. Worse still, if she was pregnant, Beppe would be digging out a shotgun.

It was time to take the initiative, not a time to sit back and vacillate over what-ifs and maybes, Rio reflected sardonically. Left in ignorance, he had dug himself into a deep hole and he had to dig himself out of it again and to do that he needed Ellie's help whether he liked it or not. Raging resentment surged up through the cracks inside him and there was no healing balm of acceptance to soothe it. Beppe was, after all, the only true family Rio had ever had, the only adult who had ever shown him love, consideration and understanding while he was still a child. And now Beppe had a daughter, whom Rio had wronged. That she could well be a money-grabbing young woman keen to feather her own nest scarcely counted now that she was about to become Beppe's heir. Furthermore, Beppe would never believe the allegations made against Ellie for there was virtually no proof of misconduct on her part.

Rio had hired a second agency to check and update the evidence he had originally been given. The hospice enquiry *had* cleared Ellie of any wrongdoing and she *had* refused the inheritance left to her by one of her patients. The only dirt left in the first investigative report relied heavily on her embittered uncle's tale about the diamond brooch and, as the police had refused to prosecute, the whole story could easily be written off as being more rumour and backstabbing than actual fact. And furthermore, if Ellie *was* a gold-digger, Rio was about to make her feel as if she'd won the lottery.

When he learned that she had checked out of the hotel he was taken aback until he noticed that her hire car was still parked outside. The receptionist told him that Ellie had walked down into the village. He found her in the cool of the ancient stone church, studying a much-admired triptych of the Madonna and Child.

When he spoke her name, she whirled round, a figure of light and movement in the dim, dark interior. Her dress was the ice blue of diamonds and the sunlight cascading through a stained-glass window high up the wall showered her in a dancing rainbow of colour that only emphasised the vibrant copper of her tumbling hair. She wasn't quick enough to hide the dismay and anxiety that crossed her face when she saw him and the tense expression and attitude that took over to stiffen her into stillness was no more welcoming.

Welcome to your biggest challenge yet, Rio thought grimly, trying not to notice how beautiful she was in that naturally beautiful way that so many women tried and failed to achieve. He froze there, suppressing his body's equally natural instincts, none of which felt appropriate in the House of God.

'Rio...' Ellie whispered uncertainly, mortified by the nerves that had stolen the volume from her voice.

He could have been carved from stone as he stood there, still and quiet as a predator, sheathed in a light grey designer suit. He resembled a stone angel with cutting cheekbones, a hard-hewn jawline and a mouth as wilful, stubborn and passionate as sin. His eyes were a pure dazzling gold in the light and she blinked rapidly, striving to shut the sheer intensity of him out and to be polite but distant, treating him the same way she usually treated men. But how could she achieve that when she knew in her heart that he had sought her out because he was shocked and agitated by what Beppe had shared with him?

'Are you a believer?' he prompted lightly.

'Yes. Are you?'

'I was raised by nuns in an orphanage and spent more time on my knees than in school. Of course I am,' Rio told her wryly.

And it was as though he had squeezed her heart at the same time as he filled in some of the blanks in her repeated attempts to understand what made him what he was. An orphanage, she thought sadly.

'I bet you were always in trouble,' Ellie remarked without thinking.

'Pretty much. Beppe and his wife raised funds for the home and did a lot to help the children, particularly the disabled ones amongst us,' Rio admitted. 'Although that home is closed now and conditions are greatly improved in its replacement. Beppe is still very much involved in finding employment and educational opportunities for the less fortunate. He is a good man.'

'Yes,' Ellie agreed tightly.

'And you are his daughter,' Rio declared without any perceptible emotion at all. 'I must assume you take after your mother since you don't look much like your father.'

'She was tall, red-haired and pale-skinned like me. I think I get my lack of height from Beppe,' Ellie breathed uncomfortably. 'You're angry that I didn't tell you why I so particularly wanted to meet Beppe.'

'It wasn't your secret to share,' Rio conceded, surprising her. 'But I must confess that I was completely unprepared for what he admitted to me. I shouldn't have been. There must have been times when he felt trapped in his marriage. He is only human.'

'Let's not talk about that,' Ellie advised. 'I don't think we can ever understand that sort of situation unless we've actually lived the same experience—'

'*Porca miseria!* That's a very compassionate comment from judgemental Ellie!' Rio commented, an ebony brow slanting up in apparent wonderment.

'Let's also try not to argue.' Ellie sent him a rueful look of appeal. 'You're shocked right now, of course you're shocked. You thought you knew everything there was to know about Beppe—'

'I don't want judgemental Ellie *or* Dr Ellie right at this moment,' Rio interposed.

The pale triangle of her face flushed as though he had slapped her. 'I'm not sure I know how to be anything else—'

'We'll have coffee…and talk,' Rio framed, extending a lean, long-fingered hand to her in invitation.

Ellie hesitated as if a shark had bared its teeth at her. And then she forced her arm to lift and she grasped his hand, a frisson of quivering awareness shimmying down her spine. He was trying to accept her and because he was making the effort, she had to make it too. His attitude thoroughly disconcerted her because she had expected only anger, condemnation and suspicion from Rio and he had just as swiftly proven her expectations wrong.

She had expected Rio to walk her across the square to the local café but instead he tucked her into the car illegally parked outside. Belatedly it occurred to her that the busy little café would scarcely be a good choice for a private chat.

'Where are we going?' she asked.

'My home. Have you had lunch?'

'No, but I'm not really hungry… Too much excitement today,' she extended wryly.

His long brown fingers flexed smoothly round the steering wheel and she remembered those fingers skimming across her body, expert and deliberate. She dragged in a short sustaining breath but she could still feel the tingling in her swelling breasts and the pulse of damp heat between her thighs. He had stripped her bare of every conviction she had once had about herself, she acknowledged reluctantly. She was a much more sexual being than she had ever dreamt but it had taken Rio to awaken and set free that side of her nature. It was terrifying to feel so vulnerable and yet Rio was currently on his very best behaviour, she recognised suddenly. Why was that? What was he planning? Why had he not yet said a single angry or insulting word to her?

'Who did this house belong to before you bought it?' she asked to break the silence as he steered the Ferrari down the long drive.

'An ancestor of Beppe's, who kept his mistress here—'

'How novel,' Ellie said drily.

'Yes, he was considered the rotten apple in the very respectable family barrel and after he died the house was left to go to rack and ruin because no one in the family thought it acceptable to live in what had once been the mistress's home. I bought it at auction and restored it. It's convenient to have somewhere close when I visit... *your father.*'

He voiced the designation with cool clarity. *Your father.* It shook her to accept that she finally had a father and that the ancestor who had kept a mistress had actually been one of her ancestors, as well. It was as though a family tree had suddenly unfolded in front of her and she smiled at the wonderful sense of security that gave her. 'I thought you would've stayed with Beppe when you visited—'

'Not if I wanted female companionship. You may not have noticed it but Beppe is rather old-fashioned in spite of his liaison with your mother,'

Rio commented. 'It's simply easier to keep that side of my life away from him.'

Ellie climbed out of the car in the sunlight, grateful to have movement to distract her from thoughts of Rio's chequered past. None of her business, she reminded herself doggedly as he led the way into the big house. A housekeeper greeted them at the door and Rio addressed her in Italian.

'I ordered a light lunch for you,' Rio told her. 'You shouldn't be skipping meals.'

Ellie compressed her lips on a hasty reply.

'And you know I'm right,' Rio added with unblemished assurance.

He guided her out to a shaded terrace and pulled out a comfortable padded chair for her. 'Sit down...'

'You're so bossy,' Ellie complained, settling down and kicking off her canvas shoes to flex her overheated bare feet on the cold stone.

His housekeeper arrived with freshly squeezed orange juice for her and a glass of wine for Rio. She wondered if she was being deprived of the alcohol option because she could be pregnant but said nothing because she had been avoiding alcohol since their moment of madness. She liked that label. A moment of madness suggested a crazy once-only impulse that was out of character, but then everything that had happened with Rio had been out of character.

'What did you want us to talk about?' she pressed boldly, not wanting him to think she was tongue-tied in his presence.

'I brought you here to propose to you but I'm not quite sure how to go about it,' Rio murmured lazily. 'If I got down on one knee, you would laugh. If I told you how much I'm worth, you would accuse me of being boorish—'

Her lashes lifted high on her bright green eyes as she stared at him fixedly. His lean, darkly handsome features were sardonic and she frowned in bewilderment. 'Propose…propose what exactly?'

Rio gazed steadily back at her, dark eyes glittering like black diamonds. 'Marriage…obviously.'

'Are you out of your mind?' Ellie gasped sharply.

'No, possibly I'm foreseeing Beppe's reaction if he discovers that I've got his wonderful new daughter pregnant,' Rio extended quietly. 'And, yes, I'm aware that we don't know as yet whether you have conceived but it would be much worse to wait and see in the current climate.'

'You *are* insane,' Ellie exclaimed, gulping down a reviving swallow of orange juice.

'Not at all. I know that Beppe will never forgive me if I've got you pregnant. He will blame me entirely for it because I have a rather raunchy reputation with women—'

'Raunchy?' Ellie rested her head to one side as if she was considering that word. 'Do you think rumours of your three-in-a-bed sexcapades have spread?'

Rio groaned out loud and sprang upright while shooting her a reproachful look. 'Can't you please put judgemental Ellie away for a while and have a serious conversation with me?'

Ellie winced. 'Not really. I can't take a marriage proposal from you seriously.'

Rio backed up against a stone pillar like a cornered lion and studied her with scorching golden eyes. 'That night in Dharia, I did not invite those women to my hotel room. They bribed their way in—'

Ellie pushed her stiff shoulders back into her comfortable seat and inclined her head. 'Oh, I guessed that,' she admitted. 'I assumed you wouldn't have double-booked yourself.'

The faintest colour scored Rio's hard cheekbones. 'You can't blame me for what *they* chose to do—'

'No, but what they did and what they assumed was acceptable said a great deal about the nature of your prior relationship with them,' Ellie pointed out with hot cheeks.

Rio swore long and low in Italian and finished his wine to set the glass down with a jarring snap on the table. 'I didn't have a *relationship* with either of them!' he fired back. 'I had sex with them on one drunken night years before the wedding. I admit that I did stuff when I was younger that I wouldn't do now—'

Her face stiff as she struggled not to betray any reaction, Ellie nodded.

'Just because you never felt the urge to experiment doesn't mean we're all the same...or that you're better than me!' Rio raked back at her.

'I don't think I'm better than you in any way. But that kind of experimentation doesn't appeal to me,' she confided.

'I can't lie and say I'm surprised,' Rio breathed, watching her like a hawk. 'Now we've got that out of the way and I can disclose that I have no plans to involve you in any form of sexual deviancy, can we concentrate on the marriage proposal?'

Ellie stiffened. 'Why would you want me to marry you?'

'If you do turn out to be pregnant I would have been asking you anyway,' Rio advanced. 'There is no way I would allow any woman to raise my child without me—'

'Rio... These days, single and separated parents are common—'

'I want my child to have everything I *didn't*

have. A home, a solid background, two caring parents, security,' Rio extended almost argumentatively. 'It's only when you don't have those advantages that you realise how very important they are.'

'I understand that and I understand how you feel,' Ellie assured him, relieved that she knew more about his background than she had. 'But there's a reasonable chance that I *won't* be pregnant—'

'I don't want to wait and take the risk that you are because Beppe will judge me for that, as well, and regard me as an unwilling husband and a very bad bet. It would be much easier just to tell him that we have fallen in love and wish to get married as soon as possible,' Rio argued. 'He will understand that and he will see nothing wrong with it.'

'I'm here on holiday,' Ellie reminded him helplessly. 'In a little over three weeks, I have to go home and return to work—'

'I will not come between you and your medical career. I own property in England and if you have to be there to complete your training, I will make that possible, whether you are pregnant or not,' he asserted.

That argument taken from her, Ellie slowly shook her buzzing head because he had taken her so much by surprise that she could barely think straight. 'So, you want to marry me to help take care of any child we might have and to keep Beppe content... Am I correct?'

'Sometimes you have the tongue of a viper,' Rio condemned in a harsh undertone. 'I want you for myself and for my own reasons and you know that! You know it every time you see me look at you, every time I touch you and struggle to *stop* touching you...'

Her pale skin flamed red at the dark liquid intensity of his deep voice. She lowered her head, finally acknowledging that she was equally out of control around him. In that they were equals. One kiss, one touch, one moment of madness wasn't enough to sate the craving. But marriage, marriage was something else entirely, wasn't it?

It was forging a future together as partners, trusting each other.

'You don't trust me,' she reminded him. 'How can you marry a woman you don't trust?'

'With care,' Rio fielded. 'You don't trust me either. Time and better understanding would take care of that. I'm sure we would both try to make the marriage a success—'

'People try that all the time with marriage and fail.'

'But there is honour in the trying,' Rio declared without hesitation. 'At least we would be doing the best we could to give our child a brighter future.'

'What if there is no child?'

'Then we eventually divorce and blame your long hours as a doctor and my business trips for keeping us apart too much,' Rio told her smoothly. 'Getting married now is a precaution for our potential child's benefit. The right start, the right environment—'

Ellie held up a hand to silence him. 'Yes, I get it but living with you would be a little like living on the side of a volcano waiting on the next eruption. You're very volatile—'

'And you're *not*?' Rio tossed back, watching her closely as her fine-boned hand closed round her orange juice to raise it to her peach-coloured mouth. 'If I had you in my bed every night I would be a lot less volatile—'

Ellie almost choked on her drink and, spluttering, set it down, her face flushing.

Rio shrugged and dealt her an amused look. 'Well, it's true. Having Beppe warn me off you doesn't improve my mood and makes it almost impossible for me to be with you.'

'We don't even have a relationship—'

'Then what *do* we have? You're splitting hairs, being too cautious. Take a risk on me,' Rio invited.

And she so *wanted* to do that, Ellie realised in astonishment. She had never done a reckless thing in her life but Rio tempted her to the edge of foolishness. What if she *was* pregnant? It would upset Beppe and mess up his relationship with Rio. It would be virtually impossible for her to manage to work and care properly for a child without a partner and a settled home. But to make that decision now when she had no idea whether or not she had conceived? She glanced up at him, at the strong face that sent her heart racing and turned her resolve to mush. Was it wise to give into that side of herself? Or would she live to regret it?

'Ellie...' Rio prodded impatiently.

'I don't rush major decisions!' Ellie responded.

Rio shot her a wicked smile. 'We could go to bed and think about it—'

'Another version of angry sex?'

'But you're not angry with me right now. You're attempting to work me out,' Rio surmised, un-coiling with fluid grace from the pillar he had been lounging back up against. 'But I'm really quite basic. If I didn't want you I wouldn't be suggesting this.'

The silence smouldered with unspoken un-dertones. In the interim, Rio's housekeeper re-appeared with a tray. A plate of delicate and ridiculously enticing little sandwiches and a pot of tea were set down in front of Ellie.

'Think of how simple all this could be...if we do it my way,' Rio urged silkily. 'We say we're in love. We marry in haste. Beppe tries to dissuade us but is secretly delighted... And a baby, if there is one...would be the icing on the cake for him.'

Ellie snatched up another sandwich, registering that listening to Rio weave his arguments with such panache and conviction improved her appetite. He had drawn an attractive picture. If she didn't marry him and then discovered she was pregnant, how much damage would she do to her new relationship with Beppe? And could she really stand by while Rio took the blame when she knew she was just as much to blame? In addition, if she was pregnant, she would definitely be seriously considering Rio's marriage proposal because no one knew better than Ellie that raising a child alone was hard. In the course of her work she had met a lot of exhausted single parents struggling to keep work and family afloat. Her grandmother had struggled with that burden, as well, and both Polly and Ellie had been made thoroughly aware of that fact.

'I'm thinking about it,' she told Rio, who was emanating a wave of silent impatience. 'I won't give up work, you know. I'll never be a trophy wife. I don't like shopping or fussing with my appearance either,' she warned him.

'I'll shop for you,' Rio countered smoothly.

'Stop being so reasonable!' Ellie exclaimed in frustration. 'I'm not used to it—'

Rio stole the last sandwich and grinned at her. 'Stop being so sensible and so negative in your outlook.'

Ellie breathed in slow and deep. 'All right... I'll do it. I'll marry you. Are you happy now?'

Rio treated her to an approving appraisal. '*Finally*. We'll go and tell Beppe straight away and I'll get my staff on to organising the wedding—'

'I have to phone my sister first...and I want to do it in private,' Ellie told him squarely, sounding a great deal more sure of herself than she actually felt.

'And then we go and buy a ring,' Rio informed her. 'We'll go the traditional route—'

'Will we?' Ellie looked at him uncertainly, for she certainly hadn't expected to be offered what she assumed to be the equivalent of an engagement ring.

Was the ring to impress Beppe with the reality of them as a couple? Or was it supposed to please her? And what was she going to say to Beppe? And how was she going to explain to Polly that she was suddenly rushing into marriage with a guy she had said she loathed?

CHAPTER SEVEN

'I JUST NEVER thought I'd see the day,' Polly carolled with a misty smile as she stepped back to scrutinise Ellie's appearance. 'You're getting married. I thought you were all set to be a spinster with a string of important letters after your name and a cat.'

Ellie had thought that too but she didn't admit it. She had never compromised on what she wanted from a man until Rio had literally crashed into her life at Polly's wedding. And that encounter had altered her image of herself and softened her rigid views. She had gradually begun to appreciate that she was lonely and that there was something hollow about achievements and more painful about trials when she had nobody to share those experiences with. Only now she was putting herself out there in a way she never had before, taking a risk on getting attached to a male who against all the odds appealed to her more than any other for no sane reason that she could find.

For Rio, she had lied for the first time in her life. She had told her father that she loved Rio but in actuality she had no idea what she felt for him. At first she had thought it was a mad infatuation but her thirst for information about him and her craving when he was absent had not faded. Surely an infatuation would have long since died from lack of fuel? All she really knew for certain was that Rio absolutely fascinated her, drew her and compelled her. And he made her feel more with him than she had felt in a lifetime of sensibly repressing strong emotions that unsettled her. And Rio had always specialised in seriously unsettling her.

She had been impressed even more when Rio had accurately forecast her father's every reaction to their marital plans and the stages of it. Beppe had initially been taken aback and had urged her not to rush into anything, but then Beppe had also confided that had he been free when he had met Ellie's mother he would have rushed to marry her. He had also admitted that he thoroughly understood the powerful life-enhancing effect of falling madly in love. And ultimately he had decided that as far as family growth went he could wish for no more than to see his daughter married to a young man he had always valued.

'Rio will grow with you by his side,' Beppe had forecast loftily. 'You make him think, you make him question what he truly wants from life. And what he has always wanted most of all is a family.'

Ellie gazed into the mirror and wondered if she was pregnant, if she could give Rio what he supposedly most wanted. But *was* that what Rio most wanted? Cavorting with all those women seemed a funny way of going about attaining a stable family life. Tomorrow morning, however, she would carry out the pregnancy test she had already purchased. She was both excited and scared by the idea. But most of all she was wondering how Rio would feel, regardless of what the result was.

She had naively assumed that she would see a great deal more of Rio once their relationship was out in the open, but Rio had flown out to Dharia to settle some complicated dispute about oil well rights and although he had urged her to accompany him and she would've loved to see her sister sooner, she had refused. Why? Girly though it was, she had wanted to work with the wedding planner Beppe had hired and make her individual choices while also being available to ensure her gown fitted perfectly. After all, she was only planning to marry once.

And her dress fitted like a dream. The corset top had been chosen with Rio in mind. She just knew Rio would revel in hooks and laces and cleavage. The long skirt skimmed down in a flattering cut over her curvy hips and fanned out below the knee. Her feet were shod in Polly's gift, a pair of enchanting high-heeled sandals studded with pearls.

'Rashad really likes Rio and the men will be

able to go off together when you visit and give us peace to gossip,' Polly remarked happily.

Ellie hid a smile because Polly was sometimes so innocent. The very last thing Ellie could imagine wanting just then was to be deprived of Rio's company. After all, he had been more absent than present since the wedding fervour kicked off. Beppe had held a series of social evenings to introduce his long-lost daughter to friends and relatives. Rio had dutifully attended those evenings before he flew out to Dharia, but Ellie's need to respect Beppe's boundaries had ensured that the bridal couple had little time alone together. Predictably, Rio had been much less accepting about the simple reality that she did not feel free to leave the *palazzo* to spend the night with him and possibly Ellie's insistence on restraint had kept him from hurrying back to Tuscany.

'When you have me wondering if we could contrive to have sex in my car without being picked up on a charge of public indecency, we have a problem, *principessa*,' Rio had complained the night before when he had joined them with Polly and Rashad for a quiet prewedding dinner. 'You need to learn to be more selfish and put us first.'

'No,' she had said. 'You need to learn that anticipation can act as an aphrodisiac.'

'But I don't need one of those,' Rio had responded with sardonic bite.

An abstracted smile tilted Ellie's lips now.

'You're nuts about him. I don't know how I didn't spot it at my wedding—'

'Your attention was elsewhere…on your bridegroom? And I'm not what you call "nuts" about him—'

'Oh, you so *are*,' Polly contradicted. 'Everything you've done just screams it, Ellie. You are not the sort of woman who meets a man and marries him within a couple of weeks unless he rocks your world…'

'People change,' Ellie argued and, eager to change the subject, added, 'isn't it really sad that we still haven't managed to find our missing sister? She could have been with us here today…'

Tracking down Lucy had so far proved difficult because she lived a travelling life, moving around a lot and surviving on casual jobs.

'We'll find her eventually,' Polly said soothingly. 'And it'll be very exciting when we do. Haven't you been tempted to look in her envelope and see what ring she was left and what name is attached to it? It could possibly help us to locate her.'

'No, I was trusted with that envelope and I wouldn't open it,' Ellie swore. 'How would you ever explain that to her when we finally met?'

'We could use steam to open it,' Polly suggested, colouring lightly at Ellie's raised brows.

'No, we should respect her privacy,' Ellie decreed.

Ellie descended the stairs smiling at her father, who stood at the foot beaming with pride. Beppe could not compliment her on her appearance enough. They travelled to the church in a limousine. She paused on the steps in the morning sunshine and she breathed in deep and slow, recognising that the elation she was feeling was happiness and marvelling at it while also fearing the undeniable storms ahead. She knew that she and Rio would argue and tussle and that there would be many times when she wanted to strangle him. That was normal life, she told herself prosaically, but true happiness was so rare a sensation for her that she wanted to make the most of it while she was feeling it.

Rio turned from the altar to get the full effect of his bride. And Ellie was stunning with her coppery hair swept up and her green eyes gleaming with intelligence above her sultry mouth. As for the dress, well, he was extremely impressed by that surprisingly sexy corset, which defined his bride's splendid curves to perfection. No, getting married didn't feel half as bad as he had dimly expected. He had thought he might feel trapped but the prospect of peeling Ellie out of that corset was more than equal to the challenge of surrendering his freedom.

Her hand trembled in his when he grasped it to thread on the wedding ring. She had worn her engagement ring on her other hand. And like Beppe's family emerald, which she had brought out to Italy with her, it was another emerald to reflect the colour of her eyes, an emerald teamed with white diamonds but not over large because Ellie didn't like flashy jewellery and had wanted something she could occasionally wear to work. So sensible, his Ellie, Rio thought wryly, wondering just when he had started thinking of her as *his*. When he'd imagined her pregnant with his child and liked the idea? When he saw her walking down the aisle towards him? Or when he realised that he was her first lover and strangely determined to be her *last*?

Of course, he knew why he was marrying her. With Ellie, the sex was on another level even though it had gone wrong the one and only time it had happened. She stood up to him, she talked back, she was his equal in every way. But more importantly she had signed a prenup contract ringed with so many iron hoops of protection that an escape artist couldn't have undermined it. If Ellie liked money, he had plenty of it and there were worse weaknesses for a woman to have, he reasoned. She could have been the unfaithful type, forever in search of the next big thrill. She could've been the uncaring, uncommitted type but he'd already seen her bonding happily with Beppe and witnessed just how close she was to her sister. And if there was to be a baby Rio was convinced that she would always and without hesitation do right by their child. The ability and the desire to be a good mother was the most imperative trait of all that a woman could have, he reflected with sombre conviction.

Ellie emerged from the church on Rio's arm. A crowd of people were crushed into the street outside. Fleeting introductions were made while the photographer fluttered around. They were congratulated and showered with rice.

In the midst of the noise and excitement, Ellie suddenly noticed two blondes wielding their camera phones and giggling like drains as they urged Rio to look at them and smile. And it was *them*, unmistakably the identical twins who had gambolled naked on Rio's bed in that Dharian hotel two years earlier. Ellie's throat convulsed. She couldn't have been mistaken, she thought angrily. They were highly noticeable women, blonde, beautiful twins, whippet thin and impossibly sparkly and effervescent in a way that was seen as ultrafeminine. Rio had actually *invited* the twins to their wedding. Ellie paled and compressed bloodless lips while the perplexed photographer urged her to smile.

She settled almost dizzily into the limousine beside Rio and looked at him. How could he do this to her? How could he be so insensitive to her feelings? Those blondes reminded her of the most humiliating moment of her life. Before Rio had opened the door to that hotel room she had been on a high, feeling like a sexy, attractive woman for the first time ever and ready to move forward, no longer feeling like the drab, clever redhead whom few men approached. And her first glimpse of the giggly twins on his bed had cut her like a knife, making her feel ridiculous and pathetic and useless.

'*Cosa c'e di sbagliato?* What's wrong?' Rio asked as the car moved off to whisk them back to the *palazzo* where the reception was being held.

And Ellie didn't know what to say. After all, he was entitled to a sexual past and in marrying him she had accepted that past. Exes at a wedding, well, not exactly what you wanted but not always avoidable either. But did the twins recognise her as the shocked woman in that doorway two years back? And would they mention that to anyone? Have a good giggle about it? She cringed inside herself and said nothing.

'Nothing's wrong,' she assured him quietly. 'It's just all the wedding hullabaloo. When it comes all together, it leaves you feeling shell-shocked.'

'I didn't invite Becky and Roz,' Rio breathed impatiently, cutting through her pretence.

So, he had noticed the twins. Well, really, how could he have missed them bouncing up and down with excitement only a few feet from him, determined to be noticed by him? Yet he had somehow contrived not to look once in their direction, nor had he shown the smallest hint of self-consciousness. But then why would he?

'Is that their names?' Ellie queried with a wooden lack of expression.

'I told the wedding planner to contact Rashad for the list of our university friends because I haven't kept up with their addresses,' Rio explained. 'They were invited to your sister's wedding and that's probably how they ended up at ours. If I'd taken a greater personal interest, I would've left them off the list.'

If anything, Ellie had grown even stiffer. 'Of course, if they're uni friends, why would you leave them out?'

'Ellie, you're putting out more sub-zero chills than a freezer,' Rio said with sardonic bite. 'But I can't change the past and neither can you.'

'I didn't realise the twins had ever been actual friends of yours,' Ellie admitted stonily, not best pleased to hear that information. 'Probably because I've never slept with any of my male friends.'

'Sadly, I wasn't quite so particular,' Rio countered in the same measured tone. 'And neither were they. In those days I could only cope with casual—'

Her smooth brow indented. 'And why was that?'

Rio squared his broad shoulders and settled back with a sigh. 'I set up a property venture when I was nineteen. Beppe was pressuring me to go to university to study business but I thought I could take a shortcut to success,' he admitted wryly. 'My business partner, Jax, had the security of a wealthy background. The property market was booming and we were doing very well, which is when I met a gorgeous brunette. I fell in love with Franca, asked her to marry me and we moved in together.'

Ellie dragged in a startled breath, for what he had just admitted was the very last thing she had expected to hear from him. After all, she had simply assumed that Rio had *always* played the field without ever pausing to settle on one particular woman. Learning different shook her up, learning that he had found that one particular woman years earlier and presumably lost her again filled her with insecurity.

Rio skimmed narrowed dark eyes over the pale,

still triangle of her face and his shapely mouth twisted. 'The property market stalled and I was overstretched. I still believe I could have made it through but Jax pulled out and hung me out to dry…and Franca, who had been screwing him behind my back and who very much liked the luxuries of life, ran off with him.'

Ellie winced and dropped her gaze, imagining the sting of that double blow of financial loss and treachery. 'I'm really sorry that that happened to you,' she murmured ruefully. 'It must've been very hard to pick yourself up after that experience.'

'It taught me a valuable lesson. At university I learned enough to ensure that I would never leave myself that vulnerable in business again,' he confided. 'I succeeded but after Franca, I avoided any kind of serious involvement with women. What the twins offered suited me at the time. No strings.'

'I can understand that,' she conceded reluctantly. 'You know…er…that night at Polly's wedding, after we parted…I've always wondered what happened—'

'You don't want to know,' Rio cut in succinctly, his tone cold as ice water.

And in telling her that he had told her everything there *was* to know, she acknowledged in consternation, just as suddenly furious with him. She had rejected him that night and had raced back to her room at the palace to take refuge in time-honoured tears and self-recriminations. But Rio had taken solace where he could find it and what right had she to object? Finding that out annoyed and disturbed her though. Rio could divide sex from emotion and treat sex like an athletic pursuit and he had done so for years before he met her. Could Rio really change? Could he switch back to the young, optimistic male he must once have been when he fell in love with Franca? And what exactly did it take to make Rio fall in love?

Rio was watching Ellie as the limo drove through the *palazzo* gates. Her delicate little profile was set, her brain running at a mile a minute on thoughts he didn't want to share. Maybe he should have lied. But lies would catch up with him sooner or later. Did she realise that she really wanted him to be perfect? Prince Charming straight out of a fairy story? And that he could never be perfect? Frustration and growing anger raged through his lean, powerful frame. He could not pretend to be something he was not in an attempt to impress her. And why would he want to anyway? Ellie would smell a rat sooner than most women because she was always looking below the surface, weighing pros and cons, picking up on inconsistencies, seeking out flaws. And he had still to confess his biggest flaw of all to a woman who had chattered animatedly about how her discovery of Beppe would now enable her to chart the previously unknown paternal half of her medical history.

In the greeting line, Becky and Roz made much of Rio and their previous acquaintance while acting as if they had never laid eyes on Ellie before. They didn't recognise her, she registered with relief, didn't remember her at all from that fleeting glimpse of her in the hotel doorway that night. But instead of being relieved at that realisation, Ellie was angry with Rio and angry with herself. She had agonised so much over that night and she had been so hurt but their backfired encounter had not had a similar effect on Rio's tough hide. She needed to guard herself from being too emotional and vulnerable around him. She had to toughen up, she told herself urgently.

Polly whisked her off after the meal. 'What on earth's wrong between you and Rio?' she demanded.

'There's nothing wrong—'

'Even Rashad's noticed the atmosphere and to be honest he's not usually that quick to notice that sort of stuff,' her sister admitted.

And Ellie spilled the whole story from its start two years earlier to the presence of the twins at the wedding. She was too upset to hold it all in any longer and Polly's shocked face spoke for her. It was several minutes before she could even move her sister on from repeatedly saying '*Both* of them?' as if she had never heard or dreamt of such behaviour before. Her attitude did nothing to improve Ellie's mood.

'And that night you met...?' Polly pressed. 'He told you that?'

'Yes, Polly,' Ellie confirmed wearily. 'I've married an unashamed man whore.'

'If Rashad had ever done anything like that, nothing would persuade him to admit it to me,' Polly declared wryly. 'But at least Rio is honest, well, brutally so.'

'I think he was just thoroughly fed up with me asking awkward questions.'

'I suspect he's already heard more than enough about that night and you shot him down in flames, which is not the sort of treatment he's used to receiving from women,' Polly pointed out grudgingly in Rio's defence. 'Let it go, Ellie. It's in the past and you weren't dating him or anything, so you can't fairly hold it against him. He didn't cheat on you. As for those blondes, ignore them, forget they're here!'

Ellie knew that was sensible advice but something stubborn in her refused to back down. Hard reality was steadily taking the bloom off her wedding day.

Rio tugged her stiff, resisting body close as he swept her out onto the floor to open the dancing. He bent his arrogant dark head and whispered, 'Do you know just how annoyed I'm getting with you?'

'Do you know how annoyed I am with you?' Ellie whispered back, unimpressed.

'Are you always going to be this jealous and possessive of me?' Rio enquired silkily.

A current of rage travelled through Ellie as hotly as a flame. 'Are you? I seem to remember you threatening to beat up Bruno for buying me dinner—'

'That was different,' Rio asserted without hesitation. 'We were already involved.'

Angry tears prickled behind Ellie's lowered eyelids and she finally knew what was really wrong with her. She had got involved with Rio on an emotional level the very first night she met him. But he hadn't got involved with her until she entered Beppe's life and became what he initially saw as a threat to someone he cared about. Was he even involved with her now that he had married her? Or had he only married her to please Beppe and because she might be pregnant? And why was she only asking herself that now and worrying about the answer?

Rio caught her hand firmly in his as they left the floor, deftly weaving them through the clusters of guests addressing them, never pausing longer than a few polite seconds. Only when they reached the foot of the main staircase did Ellie question where he was taking her and she tried to wrench her hand free.

'We're going to sort this out in private,' Rio delivered in a driven undertone.

'There's nothing to be sorted out,' Ellie protested, trying once again and failing to free her fingers from his.

Determined not to be sidetracked, Rio headed for the opulent guest suite where Ellie had dressed for the wedding. He thrust the door shut behind him in a movement that sent dismay skimming through Ellie. She had not expected Rio to turn confrontational because she had assumed that the presence of their guests would control and inhibit him. The message she was getting now was that Rio's temper was rarely repressed.

He dropped her hand and Ellie immediately made for the door. 'We can't do this in the middle of our wedding,' she argued.

Rio cut off her escape by stepping in front of the door, which in turn sent Ellie stalking and rustling angrily in all her finery across the room towards the window. She flipped round, colour accentuating her cheekbones, green eyes very bright and defiant.

'It's our wedding and it's almost over and we can do whatever we like,' he told her grittily.

'Do you have an off button?' Ellie asked helplessly. 'Because I think it's time to hit it. Yes, this is our wedding and we have had a slight difference of opinion but I have done and said nothing anyone could criticise—'

'I'm criticising you!' Rio bit out harshly.

Ellie stared at him in shock, her lips falling open, because once again, Rio was blindsiding her and catching her unprepared. He had the most amazing eyes, stunning dark gold fringed with black curling lashes, and for a split second she was held fast by them while noting the aggressive angle of his strong jaw line, the faint black stubble already shadowing his bronzed skin and, finally, the ferocious determination stamped into his amazing bone structure.

'I'm not perfect, Ellie, and I'm never going to be but I was prepared to give this my best shot—'

'I never expected you to be perfect, for goodness' sake!' Ellie spluttered uncertainly as she moved warily back towards him. 'Look, maybe I was a bit oversensitive but there's absolutely no need for us to start having this out now! Let me go back downstairs before anyone notices we're missing—'

'No,' Rio breathed with finality.

'You don't just tell me no like that and expect me to take it!' Ellie argued furiously, trying to push him away from the door.

'I keep on hoping that you'll learn from experience,' Rio growled, scooping her up, nudging a giant vase of flowers out of his path and planting her down squarely on the marble-topped side table behind her. 'But you never do.'

'This is getting ridiculous. Let me down,' Ellie told him forcefully.

Rio pinned her in place even more effectively by pushing her knees apart and stepping between them to wedge himself even closer.

'You may be physically stronger but you can't bully me,' Ellie informed him tartly.

'I don't want to bully you, *principessa*. I want you to start using your brain,' Rio bit out impatiently, settling his big hands down on her bare shoulders. 'It's time to put sulky, moody Ellie away, ditch the negativity and look forward.'

'I am neither sulky nor moody,' Ellie pronounced with as much dignity as she could summon while seated as she was on a table, being held still. His hands were hot on her bare skin, sending odd little prickles of awareness travelling through her.

'Bear in mind the fact that I'm not sulking about having had to marry a woman who *could* be a scheming little gold-digger,' Rio urged, stunning her with that statement as his long fingers flexed expressively over her shoulders.

Her lips opened. 'A…a *gold*—'

'But I gave *you* the benefit of the doubt. When do you extend the same privilege to me?' he demanded grimly.

Ellie tried to slide off the table but he forestalled her. Flushed by the undignified struggle and enraged by the label of gold-digger, she snapped, 'Let me go!'

'No. I'm keeping you right where I can see you and we're having this out right now,' Rio decreed.

'How *dare* you call me a gold-digger?' Ellie slung at him an octave higher.

'What else am I going to call you when you still haven't explained yourself? You see, I may not be perfect, Ellie but the news is that *you're* not perfect either. You've had serious allegations made against you and although I'm now aware that an enquiry dismissed one set, there are still others in your background made by a family member,' Rio reminded her caustically. 'But I was prepared to overlook that history to marry you and give you a fair chance.'

Ellie had frozen where she sat and she didn't know what to say or even where to begin. 'You said you'd *had* to marry me,' she said, instead of tackling his accusations head-on. 'But you didn't have to. I didn't demand it. I wouldn't have allowed my father to demand it either. It wasn't necessary—'

'It was necessary to me,' Rio cut in ruthlessly. 'I could not live with the chance that you could be pregnant. I had to ensure that we were a couple and that if there is a child, he or she will not grow up without me.'

'So, this really is a shotgun marriage,' Ellie breathed painfully.

'No, it's what we make of it and so far you're doing your best to undermine us,' Rio condemned.

'You know the enquiry cleared my name,' Ellie reminded him sharply. 'How can you still think I could be a gold-digger?'

'It's all those shades of grey that lie between

black and white,' Rio commented reflectively. 'What was your true intent when you befriended that old lady at the hospice where you were working?'

'I didn't befriend her. I was doing my job, acting as a sympathetic listener when there was nobody else available!' Ellie told him angrily.

'Maybe you would've got away with that inheritance had a complaint not been lodged against you and maybe you thought you could get away with it. Maybe you only looked up your father after you found out that he was a reasonably affluent man,' Rio murmured lethally. 'Who can tell? That's what I mean about shades of grey. How can I know either way? But I still took a chance on you—'

Ellie relived the stress and worry she had endured when quite out of the blue, one of the patients she had been tending had altered her will and left her estate to Ellie instead. It had been wholly unexpected and she had not felt in any way that she deserved that bequest. She had reported it immediately but naturally the old lady's nephew had lodged a complaint. It had been a nasty business and there had been nothing she could have done to avoid the ordeal. Rage and distress over Rio's suggestions roared through her taut body. 'I hate you!' she gasped chokily.

'No, you don't. You just don't like being questioned and judged without a fair trial but it's exactly what you do to me,' Rio condemned levelly.

'I don't want to be married to you!' Ellie slung at him wildly.

'You don't mean that,' Rio assured her, the hands on her shoulders smoothing her delicate skin as he bent his head. 'You want me as much as I want you.'

'Stop telling me what I want, what I think!' Ellie exclaimed in seething frustration.

'Maybe I'm talking too much… Maybe I should be *showing* you,' Rio husked, tipping her back a little and burying his mouth hotly in the smooth slope of her neck while his hands delved beneath her skirt and swept up over her thighs.

'*Stop it!*' Ellie hissed, struggling against the great wave of quivering weakness that assailed her as the heat of his lips and the teasing nip of his teeth grazed her sensitised flesh. 'You're not allowed to do this when we're fighting!'

In answer, Rio crushed her angrily parted lips beneath his own, his tongue flicking the roof of her mouth and tangling with her own. The forbidden pulse at the heart of her pounded faster and hotter while honeyed liquidity pooled in her pelvis. His hands firm on her thighs, she squirmed on the table.

'Rio!' she cried in frustration.

He ripped the delicate panties out of his path and traced the damp wet folds between her parted thighs, and so much excitement surged up inside Ellie that she feared she might go up in flames. He had distracted her, she knew he had distracted her with sex and she knew she had to defend herself but in that instant nothing was more important to Ellie than the fierce, urgent demands of her own body.

'We *can't...*' she moaned for her own benefit as much as his.

Rio sank his hands below her hips and lifted

her to him as though she were a doll. He sank into her hard and fast and the sudden fullness of him boldly stretching her made her shudder and gasp. And then he moved with brutal efficiency, hitting some magical spot inside her that knew no shame and the treacherous excitement came in a drowning, remorseless flood that overwhelmed her. Her teeth dug into the shoulder of his jacket, her hands clawed any part of him she could reach. The pleasure was unbearable, pushing her relentlessly to the edge. Her body careened into a teeth-clenching climax that left her bereft of breath and he freed her as the final convulsions trammelled through her weakened body.

He disappeared off to the bathroom leaving her sagging on the table. He had taken precautions this time around, she registered in surprise. So, he was no longer willing to take that risk of conception with her, even though they were now married. Did Rio *still* want an escape route? Was he hoping she wasn't pregnant? That he could still walk away?

And why wouldn't he when he was convinced that she was a shameless gold-digger? Anger sizzled through Ellie. She had lost another battle with Rio. She slid, almost limp with satiation, off the table and retrieved one of her shoes, which had fallen off. Her torn underwear was nowhere to be seen and she had no spare clothing in the room since her suitcase had already been removed. With a grimace she smoothed down her dress and staggered slightly on cotton-wool legs in front of a mirror to check her hair.

'You look fantastic, *principessa*,' Rio said huskily, lazily, catching her hand in his. 'And you're my wife now—'

'Not sure I want reminding of that right now—'

'I *like* reminding you,' Rio murmured, studying her with hungry dark golden eyes. 'Smile, Ellie—'

'No, Rio—'

'Smile,' Rio insisted. 'It's our wedding day and we should be making the most of it—'

'Oh, I think you've already done that,' Ellie

told him before she could think better of that comment.

And Rio laughed with unholy amusement. 'You're mine. I needed the proof of it.'

All shaken up and fizzing with conflicting feelings and emotions, Ellie returned to the wedding festivities. Rio kept a hold of her, not letting her stray far from his side. Her body still felt hot and alien, the aftershock of forbidden pleasure and excitement still trapped inside her like a shameful secret. There was wanting and then there was wanting Rio, and he had just taught her that she was the one without the off switch when she needed it. That knowledge made her feel achingly vulnerable.

CHAPTER EIGHT

RIO SCOOPED HER out of the helicopter with precision. The flight had taken less than an hour.

'Why won't you tell me where we're going?' Ellie demanded.

'In a few minutes you'll know exactly where we are—'

'I wouldn't bet on that. I haven't travelled much,' Ellie admitted as he walked her a few steps down a quay and assisted her into a motorboat.

But as he had forecast, Ellie recognised where she was even though it was a place she had only previously seen in pictures. The view of Venice as the boat sped across the lagoon was breathtakingly beautiful. 'It's just like the paintings Beppe showed me,' she whispered, entranced.

On the Grand Canal, the boat slowed amidst the

busy water traffic and nosed in at a smartly dec-
orated landing stage. Climbing out, she accom-
panied Rio into a magnificent foyer ornamented
with huge Venetian glass chandeliers. 'Welcome
to the Hotel Palazzo Sorrentino,' Rio murmured.
'The jewel in the crown of my hotel chain.'

'Sorrentino?' she queried in surprise.

'Yes, it once belonged to your family but it
was last used as a home by your great-grandfa-
ther and even he only lived in a tiny corner of it.
Beppe was quoted millions for the repairs that
were needed and he sold it to me,' Rio explained.
'It was being used as a warehouse by then because it wasn't fit for habitation. Converting it
into an exclusive hotel took years but it was a
worthwhile investment. Now it's fully booked
years in advance.'

Recognising that almost every eye in the reception area was on them, Ellie went pink, suddenly
conscious of her wedding finery. A little man in
a smart suit approached to welcome them and
handed her a beautiful bouquet with the com-
pliments of the staff. Rio accepted a key from

him and guided her across the foyer and down a corridor.

'We're staying here?' she asked.

'Not in the hotel. The *palazzo* came with a couple of attached buildings and I retained one of them for personal use. Beppe uses it regularly. He loves Venice, particularly in the winter when it's quiet,' Rio told her, leading her outside and along a wisteria-clad walled alley to a narrow door flanked by Venetian gothic windows. 'It's very private here and the staff service it so we don't have to worry about housekeeping or cooking.'

Ellie walked into a charming wood-panelled reception room that overlooked a tiny lush green garden at the rear. Beyond the garden, a gondola sailed past on a narrow waterway. It was a magical scene.

Rio removed the bouquet from her hold. 'I'll stick the flowers in the sink.'

Ellie knew she should go with him and deal with the flowers but the diverse traffic flowing past on the canal commanded her attention and she stayed where she was.

'I'll show you round now,' Rio said lightly, and in a great gilded antique mirror she caught a glimpse of her answering smile that softened her face, and looked away again, dismayed that she could look happy in the company of a man who had implied that she could be a gold-digger.

'I need to tell you about Violet... The lady in the hospice, who changed her will in my favour,' she said tightly.

'Not now, we've had enough stress. Leave it until later,' Rio urged as he opened the door on a dining room where food already awaited them on the table, fearful that any sudden revelations from Ellie would set them at odds again on a night that he very much wanted to be special and all about 'them.' 'We should eat first. You didn't have much earlier.'

'I wasn't hungry,' she admitted as he pulled out a chair for her. 'I didn't think you'd notice—'

'I notice everything about you,' Rio incised drily.

'If that was true, you'd know I'd never have sought out Beppe simply because he was well off,' Ellie contended uncomfortably. 'It didn't matter who or what he was. I just wanted to fill in the blank I've lived with all my life and know what happened between my parents. You couldn't possibly understand how much it means to me to know who my father is and to actually feel a sense of connection with him. It's so much more than I ever hoped to have.'

'I understand a lot more than you appreciate,' Rio countered, his lean dark face setting into grim lines. 'I will never know who my father is and, frankly, I don't *want* to know. I met my mother as an adult and that killed off any sentimental delusions I might have had. My mother and I didn't have a single thought or feeling in common.'

Ellie studied him in shock at that revelation.

'You were very lucky to find a man like Beppe waiting at the end of your identity trail,' Rio remarked wryly.

He had met his mother and it hadn't worked

out? But he had grown up in an orphanage. Where had his mother been when he was a child? And why didn't he know who had fathered him? Consternation gripped Ellie and she veiled her eyes. Rio managed to be incredibly sanguine about realities that would have seriously disturbed her and it made her all the more aware of how very little she knew about him and how unwittingly tactless she must have been while she was happily rambling on about what finding Beppe had meant to her. Of course, what had she ever personally shared with Rio? Discomfiture filled her. As a rule, Ellie was reserved and she kept her secrets close. She didn't share personal stuff except with Polly but that had to change now that she was married. Didn't it? It wouldn't be fair to expect more from Rio than she was prepared to give herself.

'Yes, I was incredibly fortunate,' Ellie agreed ruefully as she took another appreciative bite of her delicious pasta salad. 'Can I ask you about something?'

'Anything...'

'Earlier when we were together, you...you used a condom,' Ellie reminded him.

'Isn't that what you wanted?' Rio responded, his ebony brows drawing together in a frown. 'If you are pregnant, we'll make the best of it but if you're not, well...it gives us more options.'

'You mean, we wouldn't have to stay together,' Ellie framed, her heart suddenly beating with a dulled thunderous thud against her breastbone.

Rio lounged back in his chair with his wine glass and settled frowning dark golden eyes on her. 'Don't put words in my mouth. I said options and I *meant* options. I believe that babies should be planned and greeted with joy on their arrival.'

Ellie nodded woodenly, thinking about the pregnancy test waiting in her case. 'I agree. The circumstances weren't ideal.'

'Ideal isn't everything, *principessa*.' A slow-burning, wicked smile slanted Rio's beautiful mouth. 'But I did notice that day at my house that the idea of getting pregnant turned you as white as a sheet. It's not a risk I'll run with you unless you ask me to...'

And how likely was that? Yet that unexpected offer soothed her in some strange way. He wasn't slamming the door in her face. He had not said that if she wasn't pregnant they would eventually separate and divorce. His outlook wasn't that simple or that final. So why was she relieved? What had she feared? She searched his lean, darkly handsome features, her mouth running dry as she struggled to look beyond the sleek dark beauty of him into her appalled reaction to the threat of being parted from him. Polly had seen what she had hidden even from herself: she had got attached, dangerously attached to Rio Benedetti. Recognising that reality hollowed her out with fear. She was afraid of getting hurt and very reluctant to want more from Rio than he was likely to give.

She went upstairs to explore and discovered a dreamy spacious bedroom swathed in opulent fabrics and a divine four-poster bed. Their luggage had arrived in advance and had been unpacked for them. Off the bedroom there was a splendid marble bathroom with sumptuous heated towels and very fancy fittings. Champagne and flowers awaited them. She filched a chocolate off the silver dish beside the champagne flutes and bit into it with so much pleasure that she closed her eyes.

'You like chocolate,' Rio said huskily from the doorway.

'Correction—I would *kill* for chocolate,' Ellie admitted with a sudden laugh.

His amusement ebbed as he looked at her, the sheer stunning elegance of her in her gown, stray copper curls showing round her hairline now, the heavier make-up she had worn for the wedding faded, a faint streak of eyeliner at the side of one eye where she had rubbed. And yet she was still so beautiful with her clear green eyes and lush pink mouth. 'I think I would kill for you,' he breathed, stunned and unsettled both by the thought and the feeling.

Unfortunately Rio was being forced to work without a script. He was out of his comfort zone. Hit it and quit it was no blueprint for a marriage or a woman like Ellie. If she was pregnant, she would be with him for a long time, he reminded himself darkly. She would make demands, the sort of demands he had never had to deal with before. She would restrict him. She would also probably and regularly drive him nuts. But on the other hand, every pleasure came with a price tag and she was clever, amusing, passionate and ridiculously sexy.

Ellie plucked the pins from hair and let the thick mass fall to her shoulders. Then she spun round. 'I need your help to get out of this,' she admitted, turning and indicating the lace ties. 'It's beginning to feel very tight.'

Rio removed his jacket and cravat and unbuttoned his shirt. He was thinking about the curves inside that corset, the wondrous curves that bad timing had forced him to neglect that afternoon. Raw hunger roared through him afresh. 'I love corsets,' he confided.

'Thought you would,' Ellie murmured a tad smugly.

He released the ties and the hooks and let the garment drop to the floor while she exhaled in relief that the constriction had gone. He kept his arms round her, dipped his mouth to the smooth slope between her neck and shoulder and dallied there, lifting his head to nip teasingly at her earlobe at the same time as he raised his hands to cup her full breasts.

Ellie rested her head back against him, tiny flames of arousal dancing over her skin as long fingers tugged and teased at her swollen nipples. She was so sensitive there that she pressed her thighs together as if she could contain the rush of damp heat at her core. He backed her down on the bed but she demurred, pausing to unzip her skirt and let it fall, momentarily forgetting that she was bare beneath.

'Memories,' Rio teased with a wicked grin, disposing of his shirt to reveal a corrugated abdomen, hard with lean muscle.

'You work out,' Ellie guessed, studying him closely, faint colour feathering into her cheeks.

'Every day. I'm at a desk too much. Ah…is that a look of approval from Dr Ellie?'

Ellie scrambled onto the bed and beneath the

smooth white linen sheet and immediately felt better about hiding her overlarge behind and sturdy thighs. She didn't think there was anything wrong with her body, she simply wished that when she had been blessed with curves she had also been blessed with more height to carry them. Rio undressed, dropping everything in a heap while Ellie watched him like a hawk, thinking that it had never occurred to her to wonder what it would be like to have her own male stripper. He had a really great body. Broad shoulders, lean hips, the inverted V of muscle running down to...*that*! Ellie stared, reddened, no longer marvelling that she had been sore in the aftermath of her introduction to sex. He wasn't small anywhere and, being Rio, he was already primed for action.

'We can do without this,' he told her, yanking the sheet back. 'I plan to make you very hot, *principessa*.'

Ellie rested back on the pillows. 'And I plan to make you equally hot,' she warned him.

Grinning, Rio came down on the bed beside

her. 'You've already achieved that...or didn't you notice?'

Ellie stroked the velvet-smooth thrust of him with wondering fingers. 'I noticed—'

'A little less of that,' he censured as she explored him.

'No, you don't get to hand out orders in bed,' Ellie told him.

And Rio laughed with startled appreciation and looked at her, the humour slowly draining from his lean dark face to accentuate the black diamond glitter of his slumberous eyes and the feverish colour lacing his exotic cheekbones. 'Am I being treated to bossy Ellie now?'

'I have more than one setting. I can't have you getting bored,' Ellie murmured intently as her hand spread over his chest. 'My goodness, I'm so pale I must look like a milk bottle beside you—'

Rio rolled over and pinned her half beneath him. 'A very, very sexy, curvy milk bottle—'

'In the mood you're in you'd find anything female sexy,' Ellie protested.

'No, you really don't get it, do you? Growing

up, you were probably too busy polishing your brain cells to look in the mirror,' Rio quipped, running a fingertip along the peach-soft curve of her lower lip. 'You have the body of a goddess and a very beautiful face. Did I mention the gorgeous hair...?'

'I hate the hair. I went through school being called "ginger,"' Ellie muttered. 'And "clever clogs."'

'But you still triumphed, *bella mia*. Passed all your exams, married me—'

'Marrying you counts as a triumph?' Ellie gasped.

'See how you feel about me in the morning,' Rio murmured with lashings of sexual assurance.

'That you're tiring me out?' Ellie teased, her fingers dancing over a smooth bronzed shoulder, enjoyment lighting her eyes for such intimacy was very new to her and unexpectedly wonderful to find.

And then he leant down and he kissed her and it was exactly what he had promised, hot and hungry and wildly intoxicating. The heat of his long, lean, powerful frame against hers sent a current of prickling awareness flying across her entire skin surface. The plunge of his tongue electrified her, sending tiny shivers darting through every pleasure receptor. Her breasts tingled and swelled, the tips straining.

His mouth roamed over her, tugging at the sensitive buds, seeking out delicate spots and lingering. He worked his way down her body to explore the most responsive place of all and her hips writhed and her lips parted on tiny cries. She had never felt so much pleasure or such a relentless drive for release. It was as if something deep within her were screaming impatiently for satisfaction. She twisted and turned, drowning in sensation, her body programmed to leap and rise to fever point at his every caress. Slowly she could feel her control being torn away from her but this time it didn't frighten her. She didn't fight, she let go, rejoicing in the strong waves of pleasure convulsing her and thrumming like a euphoric song through every skin cell.

'You're really, really good at that,' Ellie whispered, limp and breathless in the aftermath.

'I'm good at a lot of things,' Rio husked, all sexual promise and dominance as he rose over her, rearranging her singing body to his satisfaction.

And if he was set on proving the fact, he proved it as he plunged into her tender depths with passionate force, reawakening her to arousal. Her heart hammered, her adrenalin kicking in as she arched beneath him, deepening his penetration, and suddenly she was greedy to experience every thrilling sensation. He moved faster, lithe and potent. Her excitement climbed with every compelling thrust. Perspiration dampened her skin, a furnace-like heat rising from the heart of her as the desire for fulfilment clawed at her. And then she was there at the summit and the blinding surge of heart-stopping pleasure seized her body and soul. She jerked and shuddered and cried out, thrown over the boundary between reality and fantasy.

Afterwards, Ellie wrapped her arms tight round Rio, feeling madly affectionate and happy.

'What are you doing?' Rio asked, tensing.

CHAPTER NINE

'I'M HUGGING YOU,' Ellie said witheringly.

'I don't do hugs.'

'I do a lot of hugging. You'll have to get used to it.' She sighed, blissfully unconcerned by his objection. She loved the hot, damp heaviness of him against her and smoothed her fingers gently down the long line of his spine. 'If I'm pregnant, you'll have a child to hug.'

She felt the charge of tension that stiffened him in her arms.

'That day...you went pale at the prospect too,' she pointed out sleepily, exhaustion weighing heavily on her.

'Of course I did. I haven't a clue how to be a parent,' Rio pointed out feelingly. 'How could I? I never had one—'

'Just like me. You'll learn as you go along,' Ellie told him drowsily, the words slurring slightly.

Rio lifted his tousled dark head. 'You can't go to sleep yet... It's our wedding night.'

But Ellie was already sound asleep. He went for a shower and eventually climbed back into bed.

Ellie wakened while it was still dark and suppressed a sigh. Her sleeping pattern had been disrupted by ever-changing shifts and a regular shortage of sufficient rest while she worked. Knowing that she was unlikely to drift off again, she got up and put on a comfy dress while scrutinising Rio as he lay sprawled in bed. He was taking up more than his share of the space, she noted without surprise. It was as well for him that he could look so good doing it, she acknowledged with tender amusement, noting the black hair curling against the pillow, the angular bone structure shaded in by stubble, the relaxed line of his mouth. Asleep he looked younger than his thirty years.

Dragging her attention from him, she went downstairs and the first thing she noticed in the sink of the elegant little kitchen was the bouquet of flowers, and guilt shot through her. A trawl through the cupboards produced a vase and she settled the blooms into water and put them on display in the sitting room. A search of the fridge revealed bottled water and savoury pastries and she ate standing up, watching the dawn light rise over the building on the other side of the canal and slowly illuminate the little garden.

'What are you thinking about?' Rio asked from behind her.

Ellie turned her head to take in Rio clad only in a pair of ripped blue jeans, his feet bare. 'Violet,' she mused wryly. 'The old lady who died in the hospice. She loved to see the dawn. If I was on duty I'd open the curtains early for her. I was thinking of how much she would have loved Venice but she never got to travel because her husband liked home best and in her day husbands ruled the roost—'

Rio grinned. 'Dare I hope it'll be the same for us?'

'Wouldn't hold my breath on that one,' Ellie advised.

'Why are you out of bed so early?'

'I've always been an early riser,' she confided. 'But then I'm not used to having the freedom to sleep in. If I wasn't working the past few years, I was studying for exams. The pressure is constant.'

Rio groaned out loud. 'Tell me about Violet while I order breakfast.'

'She was lonely. She'd outlived everyone who mattered to her,' Ellie told him. 'She had no visitors. Her nephew came once when she first entered the facility but he didn't come back. Some relatives can't handle the last stages of a terminal illness. You can't judge them for it. We're supposed to stay detached...and I never thought I'd have a problem with that.'

'Sometimes you get involved whether you want to or not.'

Ellie squared her slight shoulders. 'When I had a few minutes free I kept Violet company. That was all. She reminisced about her past and

I would listen and it made her happy. Once she was asleep I would tiptoe out again. I knew nothing about her changing her will until her solicitor contacted me after her death,' she admitted. 'I couldn't have accepted anything from her anyway because it's against the rules of the trust that employed me for medical staff to make a financial gain from patients. Even though I'd turned it down, the nephew made an official complaint against me and the whole business dragged on for months before it got to the enquiry stage and I was officially cleared. Why would I have wanted her money anyway?'

'What do you mean?'

'Rashad and Polly insisted on paying off my student loans but they also tried to persuade me to accept a large lump sum off them to buy a property. It was very generous of them but I turned it down because, while I can deal with the extravagant gifts they insist on giving me, I don't want to be the family charity case,' Ellie admitted ruefully. 'Polly buys all my clothes as it is, but she's married to Rashad and I'm not. That's *her* life, not mine.'

'And now you've got a life with me,' Rio murmured, tugging her backwards into the circle of his arms.

'I'm not sure how much of a life I can have with a man who thinks I'm after his money.' Ellie sighed just as a loud knock sounded on the front door.

Without responding to that leading comment, Rio went to answer it.

It was a waiter with a covered trolley and at Ellie's instigation it was wheeled out to the small patio, which was now bathed in early morning sunshine. The screening shrubs in the garden gave it all the charm of a forest glade.

Ellie poured the coffee. 'So now you know about Violet. It was a storm in a teacup but it had long-lasting repercussions. Mud sticks. People I trusted made nasty comments. I was worried it would damage my career and I got very stressed.'

'Naturally,' Rio conceded, wondering why it hadn't occurred to him that, had she been mercenary, Ellie could have chosen to rely on her seriously rich brother-in-law for financial support. Rashad was very generous and very family-orientated. Had she so desired, Ellie could have given up work and lived the life of a rich socialite. Why had that very obvious fact never crossed his mind at any stage? Had he preferred to think of Ellie as a gold-digger? And if so, why was that?

'That's why this break in Italy was so important to me. I needed a holiday—'

'And instead you got me—'

A natural smile tilted Ellie's lips as she looked at him, lounging back shirtless in his seat, a beautiful, self-assured and ruthless work of art, who continually surprised her. 'Yes, I got you.'

'When do we find out whether or not you're pregnant?' he prompted without warning.

'I was planning to do a test now,' she confided.

'For *yourself*?' Rio queried in visible consternation. 'No, that won't do at all. We'll go and see a doctor, get it done properly—'

'I am a doctor—'

'*Sì...*' Rio gave a fluid, very Italian shrug '...but this is an occasion and it requires special treatment.'

Midmorning, following their visit to a very charming private doctor, they sat down to coffee and pastries in the atmospheric Piazza San Marco. Both of them were shell-shocked, Ellie most of all, because she had believed she would recognise some tiny sign and somehow *know*. But she hadn't known, hadn't recognised anything that different with the exception of being more tired than usual, and with all the fuss of the wedding that hadn't seemed worthy of note.

'So, now we know,' Rio pronounced without any expression at all.

And Ellie recognised the dazed light in his eyes and knew that he was just as stunned as she was to learn that he was going to become a parent in a few months.

'I just didn't really think it could happen that... *easily*,' he admitted in an almost embarrassed undertone.

'I've met a few distressed teenagers who made

the same assumption,' Ellie admitted, smiling to herself, quietly pleased with the knowledge that she was carrying her first child. And no, their baby hadn't been planned and was likely to drive a horse and cart through her career choices, but neither of those facts mattered when set beside the wonder of conception, which she had watched give such great joy to Polly and Rashad. She would gladly make space in her life for her child, she acknowledged, recognising that in the blink of an eye after hearing that news that her goals had changed.

'Saying we would make the best of this development if it happened wasn't the most supportive or sensitive approach,' Rio conceded belatedly. 'I want to celebrate now but not only can you not drink, you've even been warned off coffee.'

There it was again, that ability to surprise her that made her love Rio all the more, Ellie reflected. In fact, loving Rio seemed to have been stamped into her genes like a no-escape clause because, of course, she loved him, didn't know quite when it had happened and certainly not *how.* She smiled, happiness bubbling through her that he was so flexible, so willing to happily embrace their unplanned baby. 'I'll drink decaf—'

Rio grimaced at the idea for he had a true Italian love of unadulterated coffee.

'There are other ways of celebrating,' Ellie pointed out, lashes screening her eyes as she covertly studied him, recognising that she would never tire of this particular view. Rio, hair blue-black and gleaming in the sunshine, stunning dark golden eyes welded to her with an intensity she could feel, sprawled back with indolent grace in his seat, his shirt pulled taut across his broad chest, his trousers straining over his powerful thighs. Her mouth ran dry.

'Eat your ice cream, Signora Benedetti. I love your curves—'

'Just as well. My curves will be expanding—'

A slashing grin curved his sculpted mouth. 'I can only look forward to it, *principessa*. But when it comes to celebrating—'

'You could take me out on a gondola,' Ellie suggested with enthusiasm.

Rio looked pained. 'Seriously uncool. That's a touristy thing—'

'Please...' Ellie urged.

And she got her gondola ride the whole length of the Grand Canal. Rio had caved and she was touched. He was much more comfortable sweeping her into a fancy jeweller's store afterwards, where he insisted on buying her an emerald pendant to mark the occasion. They lunched back at the house and he watched her smother a yawn.

'You should lie down for a while—'

'Only if you lie down with me,' Ellie murmured softly.

Disconcerted, Rio flashed her a glance as if he couldn't quite credit the invitation. But without hesitation he lifted her up out of her seat and crushed her ripe mouth under his own, all the seething passion of his intense sexuality rising to the fore.

He tumbled her down on the bed but he unwrapped her from her clothes like a precious parcel, pausing to admire and tease what he exposed, and she writhed like a wanton on top of the silk bedspread in the full glare of the Venetian sunlight, utterly lost in passion and equally lost to all shame. He took her from behind then, hands firm on her overheated body as he drove into her with a roughened growl of satisfaction. His urgent rhythm was wildly exciting. Heart pounding, breathing forgotten, Ellie reached a peak and her body detonated in an explosive charge of pleasure. She slumped down winded on the bed with Rio on top of her.

He released her from his weight and settled down beside her, reaching for her to pull her into his arms.

'Thought you didn't do hugs,' Ellie commented.

Rio splayed a large hand across her flat stomach and said piously, 'I'm hugging my child.'

Ellie laughed, feeling amazingly relaxed and at peace. Her fingers lifted and fiddled absently with the emerald she still wore round her neck.

'You can tell me about your uncle now,' Rio informed her in the tone of someone doing her a favour.

Ellie wrinkled her nose. 'Jim Dixon? My mother's brother? I guessed he would be the family member you mentioned. I take it he's still peddling his sob story about how I ripped him off?'

'You're not surprised?'

'Jim's vilified me everywhere and no matter what I said to him, he refused to listen. He doesn't *want* the truth. He didn't get on with my mother and he never liked Polly and me, but my grandmother was living on the poverty line when she agreed to raise us. Our mother gave her a lot of money to take care of us and the arrangement suited them both from that point of view. Unfortunately my uncle always resented us being there.'

'Tell me about the brooch,' Rio urged with typical impatience.

'Oh, the *famous* diamond brooch, the family heirloom for several generations and the only item of worth the Dixons ever owned,' Ellie recounted ruefully. 'My grandmother sent me a letter during my first term at medical school. In it she told me she wanted me to have the brooch because she was so proud that I was going to be a doctor. She gave it to me the first weekend I was home after that. I didn't tell Polly, well, I couldn't *bear* to—'

Rio had sat up, glorious dark eyes locked to her expressive face and narrowing. 'Why not? I thought you and your sister were really close.'

'Oh, come on, Rio, think about it! Polly was the eldest and the brooch should have gone to her if it had gone to anyone!' Ellie argued. 'Polly sacrificed her chance to go to art college to get a job and help out financially and when Gran developed dementia, it was Polly who looked after her. She deserved the brooch, *not* me, and I was astonished enough to get it because our grandmother wasn't a warm woman. She didn't neglect or abuse us but she didn't love us either. Polly would've been hurt by me getting the brooch, so I decided to sell it and split the proceeds with her and make up some story about where I got the money from.'

'Women… Why do you always complicate things?' Rio groaned. 'A man would just have told the truth. It wasn't your fault that your grandmother chose to give it to you.'

Ellie rolled her eyes, unimpressed. 'But when I tried to sell the brooch, I discovered it was only paste, not real diamonds, which made better sense to me. I mean, why *would* a poor family have held on to a valuable diamond brooch all those years? It was worth so little that I didn't bother selling it but I still haven't told Polly about it,' she completed guiltily.

'Where does your uncle come into this?'

'Our grandmother left her son the contents of her house when she died and, of course, he assumed that the brooch would be there and when I told him she'd given it to me a couple of years earlier, Jim accused me of being a thief. While Polly was out applying for the death certificate and making burial arrangements, I was wrangling with Jim. I told him the brooch was only a costume piece but he wouldn't believe me and he stomped off and wouldn't speak to us at the funeral. A few weeks later he got the police involved,' she revealed wryly. 'They came to see me at university. I showed them the letter. They were satisfied—'

'But your uncle wasn't?'

'No, he'll probably go to his grave convinced that I deprived him of his prized inheritance. I tried to sort it out with him and he wouldn't listen and by that stage I was past caring. I was sick and tired of the whole stupid business,' she confessed.

Rio traced a fingertip over the shadows below her eyes. 'You look tired, *principessa*. Have a nap.'

He owed her an apology for having entertained the ridiculous idea that she could be a gold-digger, Ellie thought in annoyance, but she was *still* waiting for that apology. He was far from perfect, she mused, and he was too strong to find it easy to own up to being in the wrong. On the other hand, he had wonderful taste in emeralds, had endured a gondola ride at her behest, was learning to hug and he was happy about the baby, she reasoned with sneaking contentment while swallowing another yawn.

Rio watched Ellie sleep and heaved a sigh. Had she noticed his moment of sheer panic when her pregnancy was confirmed? His blood had run cold. He had asked himself how he could possibly be a decent parent when his own parents had had more in common with the dregs of humanity. He didn't know what was in his genes, never would know, but that sort of stuff was important to Ellie. Was that why he *still* hadn't told her about the dumpster? Pride? He had always told himself that where he started out didn't matter; indeed that all that really mattered was where he ended up.

And where had he ended up? Married to a woman he had treated badly! His sins had come back to find him out and haunt him. So, he had to reinvent himself again, just as he had as a boy, as a young failed businessman, a student and, finally, a success story. He would change and adapt to his new lifestyle. He would be *the perfect husband*. That was what Ellie deserved. He owed her that. All her life, Ellie had only had her sister Polly to rely on but now she had him. He smoothed a corkscrew curl back from her pale brow, careful not to wake her, and abstractedly wondered if it would be too soon to visit a toy shop. Probably as uncool as that awful gondola ride, he conceded ruefully. But then wasn't he supposed to be reinventing himself?

'So how do you think my Italian is coming on?' Ellie enquired in the language.

'You are learning quickly and the accent, it is good,' Beppe told her cheerfully. 'Rio must be a better and more patient teacher than I expected.'

'He's been very patient but we only talk in Italian for a couple of hours a day. I find it exhausting,' she admitted. 'But I have a good memory. Outside of maths and science, languages were my best subject.'

'When will you be home?' Beppe asked plaintively. 'I miss you both.'

'Tomorrow. We'll join you for dinner,' Ellie promised and she finished the call because Polly had already texted her twice asking her to ring.

'What's happened?' she asked her sister worriedly minutes later.

'You *have* to open Lucy's envelope,' Polly told her and then she explained why and Ellie came off the phone again looking worried.

'What's wrong?' Rio pressed, lifting his handsome dark head from his laptop.

'Well, that kid sister we've been trying to find?' She sighed. 'It turns out that we didn't really think things through properly at the start. Because we didn't know who our fathers were, we assumed Lucy would be in the same boat. But Lucy's had access to her original birth certificate since she was eighteen and her father's name is probably on it. After all, he was living in London with our mother when she was conceived. All the investigator has been able to discover from enquiries is that Lucy's father is Greek and he thinks it's possible that the reason we can't trace her is that she could be in Greece.'

'That's reasonable, so stop fussing and open the envelope. It's only a name and a ring, nothing more important.'

'It just feels wrong,' Ellie muttered, going upstairs to extract the envelope from her case and clattering back down into the sitting room. She opened the envelope and extracted a ruby ring and read the name. 'Kreon Thiarkis,' she sounded out uncertainly.

'I think I've heard that surname before. I'll look into it. Text the name to Polly so that she can pass it straight on to the investigator,' he urged unnecessarily because she was already doing exactly that.

'Stop with the bossy stuff,' she warned him.

'Have you ever listened to yourself talking to Beppe? Telling him to eat more vegetables and drink less wine? Urging a man, who is physically very lazy, to go for walks? It's not going to kill him to be a little overweight at this stage of his life,' Rio opined. 'You climb on your healthy-living soapbox every time you're on the phone.'

Ellie winced. 'Have I been overdoing it?'

'No. Beppe enjoys being fussed over. He's never had that before. And if it's any consolation, you're giving him very good advice but he's very set in his ways.'

Afternoon tea was served to them out in the little garden and Ellie sat watching the canal traffic wend past in all its tremendous variety while she ate a divine slice of blackberry-limoncello tart. She was thinking about how very happy she was and that it seemed downright incredible to her that she had only been married for four short weeks.

After all, she had made some very major decisions during those four weeks. Finding Beppe, marrying Rio and discovering she was pregnant had forced her to have a serious rethink about her future. She had withdrawn at the last minute from her scheduled placement in London and was officially unemployed. But she was learning Italian as fast as she could and with Rio's assistance had already collected up the documents required for her to register as a doctor in Italy. Her career wasn't taking a back seat, she reasoned, she was simply on a go-slow diversion for a few months. Obviously, her priorities had changed.

She didn't want to leave Italy now that she had found her father. With Polly married to Rashad and living in Dharia, she had no family waiting for her back in London. She wanted the time and the space to get to know Beppe, as well. And she loved Italy and saw no reason to demand that Rio live in the UK when it was perfectly possible for her to work in Italy. That decision had removed much of the stress and the fear of the future weighing her down.

And she was so happy with Rio, even though he was the sort of near-workaholic who brought his tablet out even for afternoon tea in the sunshine. They had still contrived to enjoy the most incredible honeymoon exploring Venice. Well, she had explored and he had guided, occasionally complaining bitterly when she dragged him into old buildings or shot what she thought were interesting historical facts at him. They had wandered hand in hand off the beaten track and eaten wonderful food at little restaurants known only to the locals.

Many a morning had drifted long past noon before they got dressed. He was insatiable or maybe she was, she reflected ruefully, but they at least seemed well matched in that field. For the first time ever Ellie was learning what it was to have time to waste, to be indolent, to read a something that wasn't a textbook or a research paper.

And throughout every step of that most entertaining renaissance of hers, Rio had encouraged her and supported her. He made her happy: it was that simple and that was probably why she loved him. They still argued though. After she had told him the story of her grandmother's brooch, Rio had made the very extravagant gesture of buying her a star-shaped brooch studded with enough diamonds to sink the Titanic. 'You *deserve* it,' he had told her while she was trying to remonstrate with him over the expensive jewellery he kept on buying for her even though she rarely wore jewellery because she had never had much to wear. Stone Age man went hunting and dragged a carcass home to his cave to feed his woman. Rio's equivalent was inviting exclusive jewellers to visit the house to show her an array of fabulous gems worth a small fortune. And if she said no, he looked frustrated and hurt, and it was the hurt she couldn't bear to see.

If she made any sort of comment relating to gold-diggers, he froze and changed the subject. No, he still hadn't apologised but she was bright enough to know that the flood of expensive jewels was Rio's way of telling her that he no longer nourished such insulting suspicions about her. And the one thing he wouldn't talk about was his time in the orphanage and his dealings with his mother as an adult. For some reason the story of his early years was a complete conversation killer.

Ellie stirred that night soon after she heard the phone ring, for working in the medical field had wired her to take greater note of alarms and phone calls. Coming sleepily awake, she sat up and watched Rio pace the floor naked. He was speaking in Italian and far too fast for her to follow, shooting urgent questions to whoever was on the other end of the call. And he was upset, lines grooved into his lean dark features, mouth a thinned tense line. Disturbed by what she was seeing, Ellie breathed in deep, bracing herself for trouble of some kind.

Rio made another call and then looked across at her with unconcealed anxiety. 'We need to go home. Beppe's in hospital. He had a heart attack while one of his friends was dining with him. He received immediate attention...which is good. *Isn't it?*' he demanded jerkily, seeking reassurance.

Ellie braced herself, fighting the strong emotions tearing at her at the very thought of losing the father she had only recently found. 'Yes, it will greatly improve his chances of making a full recovery,' she muttered hollowly, striving and failing to be more upbeat.

CHAPTER TEN

'SILLY FUSS,' BEPPE said again as Ellie gripped his hand. 'No reason to come back early.'

Even though Ellie was no stranger to the environment of an Intensive Care Unit, she was having a first-hand experience of how very intimidating it could be to see someone she loved lying in a railed bed, and Beppe looked so small and shrunken. She breathed in deep and slow, composing herself, because she was determined not to inflict more pressure on her father by over-reacting.

Beppe had had an emergency angioplasty to clear a blocked artery soon after his arrival at the hospital and his prognosis was good if he followed the rules on how best to maximise his recuperation. But her father's heart attack had given him a terrible fright because he had not spent even a day in hospital before and had enjoyed excellent health.

Rio, however, had suffered an even worse fright, Ellie acknowledged. For during the flight that had whisked them back to Florence in time to see the dawn, Rio, sky-high on anxiety, had sat lost in his thoughts and barely speaking. Right at that moment he was poised at the foot of Beppe's hospital bed trying to act strong and optimistic for Beppe's benefit but Ellie could spot a pretence when she could see one. One of Rio's hands was clenching and repeatedly unclenching in a betrayal of stress that could not be hidden. And for the first time—and she scolded herself thoroughly for it being the first time—she finally recognised that Rio loved Beppe as much as she did, indeed probably more because Beppe Sorrentino had been a part of Rio's life since he was a child.

'Want to live to see grandchildren,' Beppe told them apologetically, his speech abbreviated and slurred by the medication. 'Never had family, want that now.'

'And you'll have that family,' Ellie assured him soothingly.

'Maybe sooner than you think,' Rio slotted in, ready, Ellie could see, to expose her there and then as a pregnant bride if it helped his godfather to look forward and raised his spirits.

'Hopefully we'll have news of that nature sometime soon,' Ellie delivered to silence Rio.

A nurse adjusted the machinery surrounding Beppe and a more senior nurse with a clipboard questioned her quietly from the doorway.

'Franca...' Beppe murmured with a weak smile in the direction of the woman in the doorway. 'Wondered when you'd visit.'

Ellie watched Rio freeze in patent disbelief and then slowly turn round. Her own brain, drained by the sleepless night and the stress, seemed to be refusing to function. The nurse in the doorway was Rio's ex? Or another Franca entirely? Could she possibly be the woman Rio had once planned to marry? The same one who had run off with his one-time business partner, Jax, when Rio's property venture failed? It was a moment when Ellie would happily have given ten years of her life to be seated in the right place to actually see Rio's face and interpret his reaction.

'Franca…' he acknowledged after a noticeable pause and he addressed her in quiet Italian, moving forward and indeed stepping outside into the corridor to speak to her at length. She was a small, fragile brunette with big dark eyes and ridiculously pretty and right at that moment she was gazing soulfully up at Rio as though he had hung the moon for her.

Beppe squeezed Ellie's limp fingers to attract her attention and her shaken eyes darted back to him. 'She's been working here for years,' he whispered. 'I knew and never said. He didn't know.'

'They're old friends though,' Ellie pointed out with forced casualness, deliberately avoiding any hint of discomfiture for the older man's benefit.

Beppe patted her hand. 'Good girl,' he mumbled. 'Sensible girl.'

Ellie watched his eyes drift shut and slowly breathed in again, feeling almost giddy as the oxygen hit her lungs. Switching her attention back to Rio and Franca, she saw a doctor joining them and she rose from her chair quickly, keen to join the medical discussion clearly taking place in the corridor. But as she straightened she lurched and stumbled, a sudden wall of blackness closing in around her. And her last thought was, *How could you be so stupid?*

Rio scooped up Ellie at such speed that he almost tripped over Beppe's bed in his haste to reach his wife. 'She's pregnant,' he announced in a panic to anyone who cared to listen.

Guilt slashed at Rio as he carted Ellie out to the waiting limousine. He had dragged her out of bed in the middle of the night and she hadn't eaten in hours. That combined with the stress of Beppe's condition had been too much for a newly pregnant woman. Why hadn't he paid more attention to Ellie's needs? As Franca had explained, Ellie was probably experiencing low blood pressure and low blood sugar at this stage.

Ellie began to try to sit up in the car, saying limply, 'What are you doing? I don't want to leave the hospital—'

'Beppe is asleep. For the moment, the crisis is over and there's no reason for you to stay by his bedside,' Rio argued forcefully. 'Right now, you need to eat and rest. And *no*,' he instructed, actually daring to rest two long fingers against her parted lips in reproof. 'Don't bother reminding me that you're a doctor when you can't remember to look after yourself.'

A furious flush mantled Ellie's cheeks. She felt the sting of his censure all the more because it was warranted. But there had been no food on the private jet because there had not been time to restock it for the emergency flight from Venice, so eating had not been an option during the flight, and since their arrival she had only seen the inside of the ICU.

'Beppe didn't see me faint, did he?' she pressed worriedly.

'No, he was fast asleep—'

'What did his doctor tell you?'

'That he's on the mend but that he needs to make the changes you mentioned.' Rio swore under his breath in driven Italian. 'I feel guilty now. I should've tried to talk to him too—'

'At the end of the day, it's his life and his decision,' she said tiredly. 'I think he'll be practical, especially once he realises the next generation is on the way, although how he didn't guess from the way you were talking I'll never know!'

'Dio mio...' Rio growled out of patience. 'We *are* talking about a man who had an adulterous affair with your mother! Beppe wasn't perfect. Why would he expect us to be?'

Ellie sniffed, still reluctant to be exposed as the loose woman who had ended up on a sofa with Rio within days of her arrival in Italy. Not even in a bed, her censorious alter ego reminded her darkly. Rio made her reckless but he also made her happy…well, when he wasn't annoying her or worrying her.

'So was that the same Franca you once planned to marry?' she simply shot at him, going straight for the jugular, in no mood to contrive a subtle approach.

Rio flexed his broad shoulders and sprawled back in his corner. 'That was a surprise but I gather Beppe knew and never mentioned it.'

'I didn't know she worked in the medical field—'

'How would you?' Rio parried. 'It's not relevant in any way.'

Ellie pursed her lips. No, it might not be relevant on his terms, she was thinking grimly, but that one little fact of Franca's nursing profession and her treatment of him could certainly shed some light on Rio's reluctance to view medical staff as being 'caring' and the suspicious reception he had given Ellie.

'How did you feel seeing her again?' Ellie asked baldly, knowing it was intrusive but unable to kill the question before it leapt off her tongue. Because, in truth, the answer to that one little question was literally *all* she wanted to know.

Rio treated her to an incredulous appraisal. 'I'm not going to answer that. It's a stupid question.'

Ellie nodded, mouth compressing harder than ever.

And Rio thought quite spontaneously that Beppe would never have got the chance to stray from his marital vows with a wife like Ellie around. Ellie picked up on every nuance, dissected it, stressed about it and absolutely had to *talk* about it immediately. And sometimes it drove Rio crazy because his brain didn't work like hers. Why would he even *want* to talk about Franca? Aside from the reality that that liaison had happened what felt like half a lifetime ago? Women discussed feelings but he had never felt that need, had he? He very shrewdly kept that kind of nonsense to himself. Why did Ellie always want something from him that he couldn't deliver? Time and time again she showed him that he was failing to meet her expectations.

His jawline setting like granite, Rio brooded about yet another major flaw in his character. He didn't know how to talk about feelings, where even to begin, never mind end. He had had lots and lots of feelings when he was a boy, but he had learned through hard experience that it was wiser and safer to suppress them. He was resolutely practical and always had been. There was no point wanting what you couldn't have and even less point in wasting energy agonising over life's misfortunes. That creed had served him faithfully for thirty years. So, how *had* he felt seeing Franca without warning? Surprise and curiosity. Nothing wrong with those reactions, was there?

'You go to bed while I make you something to eat. What would you like?'

'You can cook?' Ellie gasped.

'Proficiently,' Rio assured her with satisfaction.

'Could you manage an omelette? Omelettes are kind of complicated, aren't they?' Ellie said in the tone of a woman who lived off salads and ready meals.

'Not that complicated,' Rio told her.

He led Ellie up to the master bedroom in his house and her luggage was brought up. She studied her surroundings with tired interest. Luxury fabrics and pale oak furniture lent the bedroom a traditional, almost feminine opulence that disconcerted her because it was very far from what she had expected to find in a rampant womaniser's intimate lair. Had she been less tired she might have noticed that Rio was scanning the bedroom, as well, in a manner that suggested he was equally unfamiliar with it.

And so he was, having hired a decorator to chuck out his man cave accoutrements and decor while they were in Venice. Everything was new, fresh and Ellie approved even though she didn't know it because he had made note of her favourite colours and the style of furniture she liked. She didn't like cutting-edge contemporary and she didn't like flashy and his former bedroom decor would have qualified in both categories. There had also been the serious risk of inadvertently encouraging Ellie to think about how many other women could have visited his home and slept in that bed. No, Rio was convinced that keeping Ellie happy meant acting as if that past of his didn't exist. He understood her passionate possessiveness, in fact, it warmed him as much as the hottest day, but he didn't want any element of his libidinous past coming between them.

And that included Franca. If he talked about Franca, he would be clumsy and he might well say the wrong thing. For that reason it was much better not to discuss Franca at all. Thinking that that was the troublesome topic of Franca now as done and dusted as a gravestone in a cemetery, Rio went downstairs to make an omelette worthy of a cordon bleu chef because he never missed out on an opportunity to impress Ellie and he had just realised that she couldn't cook.

As removed from the real world as a zombie, Ellie opened her case, extracted the necessities and went into the bathroom. She had a quick shower, discovered she had left her toothbrush behind in Venice and searched the drawers in the storage units. She found several new toothbrushes, a giant box of condoms, a choice of several different lipsticks and make-up containers and two unmatched earrings. All had clearly been left behind by previous visitors. Tomorrow she would dump them. Right at that moment, she was reminding herself that Rio was her husband, that, yes, he had had a past with other women, but that that was nothing to do with her, certainly not something she should be worrying about.

Rio presented her with a perfect golden omelette and she was undeniably as impressed as though he had owned up to being a rocket scientist. Washed and fed, she was taken over by exhaustion again and she slid down in the blissfully comfortable bed, quite unaware that Rio went for a shower and then slid in beside her.

When she wakened it was afternoon the next day and she was alone. She was shocked that she had slept so long and anxious to get to the hospital and see how her father was doing. When she came downstairs, Rio's housekeeper appeared, introduced herself as Sofia and brought her lunch on the terrace. Marooned without transport, she went into the large garage off the rear courtyard and discovered a stable of vehicles. Rio liked sports cars, she thought with amusement. *Boy*, did Rio like sports cars. Sofia showed her where the keys were and she picked a car in fire-engine red that appealed to her mood.

Navigating the many turns in the sweeping road that led down to the main route was more of a challenge than she had expected because she had never driven such a powerful car before but she made it to the hospital in good time and went straight to the ICU. Beppe, however, had been moved out of intensive care to his own room, a sign that he was making good progress, and she greeted him with a smile when she found him sitting up in bed and much more able to talk than he had been in the early hours of the morning.

'Rio's gone for coffee in the canteen,' he explained. 'You've just missed him.'

After she had been with him about thirty minutes, Beppe began to flag and she suggested he have a nap, reminding him when he argued that he was recovering from surgery and that it would take a few days for him to regain his strength. Ellie went straight down to the canteen in the basement to find Rio but it was very busy and she bought herself a cup of hot chocolate as a treat, while she queued and scanned the crowded tables.

When she finally located him, she stopped midway on her path to joining him because he was not alone, he was sitting with Franca. Reluctant to interrupt out of the fear that Rio would deem it jealous and possessive behaviour on her part, Ellie slid into a corner table nicely shielded by a tall fake potted plant and waited for his companion to leave. She barely sipped her hot chocolate while she watched the pair of them, former lovers, looking much more friendly than anyone would have expected in the circumstances as they sat opposite each other, both leaning forward to get closer and talking intently.

In not treating Franca like an enemy, Rio was acting like an adult, she told herself soothingly. It was downright nasty of her to think that Franca was looking at him with much more appreciation than the occasion could surely require. Slowly it sank in that they appeared to be having a quite emotional conversation and that unnerved her, but all the signs were there. Franca reached across the table and gripped one of Rio's hands at one point and then brushed away tears. Rio did not go into retreat. In fact, none of the barriers that most would expect to be present between lovers who had parted on very bad terms were to be seen.

Stop being so blasted jealous and suspicious, Ellie urged herself in exasperation. Obviously Rio and Franca were catching up on the past and had discovered that at heart they were still friends. But it really, *really* bothered Ellie that Rio was clearly having the sort of emotional chat with his ex-girlfriend that he refused to have with his wife. And for how long had he been chatting to Franca? All that time she had been upstairs sitting with Beppe? And he was *still* with her?

Ellie drank her hot chocolate, refusing to allow herself to watch Rio and Franca any more since she was obviously too susceptible to paranoia.

She had fallen insanely in love with Rio, married him and turned into a maniac she didn't recognise. Every hour of the day she wanted Rio *so* much. It was frightening, mortifying, but she had to get control of her craving, her suspicions, her insecurity. One last look at them and then she would go and check on Beppe again, she bargained with herself.

And Ellie glanced, only allowed herself that one glance, and she saw Rio reach over the table to grip Franca's hand in a heartfelt gesture that felt like a knife plunging into her own heart. Franca put one of her hands on top of his and gave him a wobbly, tearful smile full of warmth and admiration. Ellie's glance became a stare and then she literally tore her gaze away at the same time as she stood up, abandoning her drink, and walked out of the canteen to wait for the lift.

Right, so, Rio had some weird new connection with his ex, not necessarily a sexual or romantic connection. Who was she trying to kid? She had sat watching a woman crying and smiling and holding hands with her husband. What was she supposed to think? A woman he had once loved enough to want to marry. But he had never loved or wanted to marry Ellie, had he? And now he was stuck in a marriage with a woman he didn't love, who was pregnant.

Ellie's eyes prickled like mad. She hardly ever cried and right at that moment she had a crazy urge to howl and sob, and holding all that pent-up emotion in was a challenge. Rio was so intense in everything he did and yet, unless he lost his temper, he didn't let that emotion escape, at least not around Ellie. But what had really seriously hurt was seeing Rio demonstrate unashamed emotion with Franca, Rio taking part in the kind of emotional exchange he had denied Ellie. So what had they been talking about?

Had they discovered that they both still had feelings for each other? Franca must have been Rio's first love and first loves, with all the memories involved, were notoriously hard attachments to shake. Ellie breathed in slow and deep to calm herself and checked on Beppe, but he was sound asleep and, according to the nurse she spoke to, likely to be for some time. There was no reason for Ellie to remain at the hospital, particularly not when she wanted to avoid Rio, who she knew very well wouldn't tell her anything about his encounter with Franca. If she taxed him he would think she was a jealous, suspicious cow and he would be right. She *was*…

As she drove off from the hospital she struggled to calm down. Only a couple of hours earlier, aside of her ongoing concern for her father, she had been blissfully happy and Beppe did seem to be improving. She was making a mountain out of a molehill, she told herself soothingly. She would say nothing, do nothing, wait and see how matters went.

But inside herself, Ellie felt as though her heart were breaking. She kept on getting a flashback of Rio holding hands with Franca, Franca staring back at him with so much brimming emotion. Was that love she had seen between them? Why not? Why shouldn't he love Franca? Seeing his former love in such a crisis as Beppe's illness had created when Rio had been in a very emotional state of mind, even though he wouldn't ever admit the fact? Had Franca and Rio recognised that they both still had feelings for each other?

And, yes, she had believed that Rio was happy with her in Venice, but what if all along from the very outset of their marriage Rio had only been making the best of things? The best of a bad job? He found her sexually attractive but was there any more to their connection on his side than that? Meeting Franca again could well have made Rio appreciate the difference between love and sex. Her stomach turned over sickly.

So *why* should she keep quiet about what she had seen? an angry voice inside her demanded.

After all, how would Rio have reacted to seeing her holding hands with another man? Rio would have gone up in flames, created a scene and demanded an immediate explanation. That was the truth of it. Rio was as hot-headed and impulsive as she was invariably sensible and cautious. So, if Rio wouldn't swallow that kind of behaviour, why should she?

Ellie drove back to the house, steadily getting more and more upset and tearful. Whatever she did, she had to make a statement. She had to make it clear that she would not tolerate any kind of flirtation because if she didn't Rio might go on doing it. He needed boundaries, no, he needed a giant wall built round him to keep him within acceptable behaviour limits, she decided furiously. So, it was better to overreact now in the hope that the fallout from her anger ensured that there would not be a *next* time, she reasoned in growing desperation.

A preventative gesture in mind, Ellie began to pack her cases again. She would move into Beppe's house for a few days and Rio would appreciate that she was seriously annoyed with him. But was that the right thing to do? What if Rio had realised he was still in love with Franca? A terrible frightening sensation of emptiness spread inside Ellie, because if she lost Rio, she felt as if she would lose everything.

And that was sad, really, *really* sad, she told herself bracingly. She loved him but that didn't mean that she intended to be a doormat or throw wild, volatile scenes whenever he did something she disliked. Walking out on him for a couple of days was a better, quieter option and he would realise that she was serious. Screaming at Rio would be unproductive because he was as stubborn as a mule.

Rio drove back to his house, still surprised that he had somehow missed Ellie at the hospital. He was in an extraordinarily good mood. Beppe was on the mend, Ellie was pregnant and certain misconceptions he had once held had been cleared up and had left him feeling more in tune with the world than he had felt in a long time. He was in the wrong place mentally to reach home and have a troubled Sofia indicate the envelope left on a coffee table while learning that his wife had departed with cases.

He tore open the envelope. It was an Ellie letter, very succinct and to the point. There was only one sentence, telling him that he had failed to demonstrate the commitment she required from a husband. What the hell was that supposed to mean? Rio swore and then he swore again. It was as if electric shocks were going off in his brain. Ellie had walked out on him and moved into Beppe's *palazzo*. Outrage roared through him. He had made a huge effort to meet Ellie's high standards and yet now she was trying to ditch him like an old shoe.

Rio reacted by doing something that Ellie had not foreseen. He phoned Rashad and asked to speak to Polly. But within a minute of speaking to Ellie's sister, he realised that she was as shocked as he was and had no idea what could have fired Ellie up to that extent.

'Ellie's really not the dramatic type,' Polly told him unreassuringly, because that only suggested that he must have been guilty of some giant sin that had provoked sudden and uncharacteristic behaviour.

'But I haven't *done* anything!' Rio raged, pacing round the hall in sizzling frustration. 'Do you think it could be pregnancy hormones or something weird?'

Polly's astonishment at that news only convinced Rio that phoning your wife's sister for insight into an unfathomable development could be a seriously bad and undiplomatic move. But then it had never occurred to him that Ellie could have kept quiet about the baby even with her sibling. After all, she and Polly talked most days! It finally dawned on him that Ellie was a much more private person in nature than he had appreciated—someone who didn't share personal stuff unless forced, as he had had to almost force her to tell him about the diamond brooch and the old lady at the hospice. She held all her distress in, *hid* it, trying to stay strong. Until that moment he hadn't recognised just how similar they were in that category and he suppressed a groan because it only complicated his situation more. Maybe she was deeply unhappy living with him. How was he to know? She wasn't a talker or an emoter... *Per l'amor di Dio*, he was *so* grateful for her restraint in that line. After all, Franca had almost talked him into a trance.

Initially, powered on anger, fear and a desperate need to take a stance, Ellie had expected Rio to rush straight to Beppe's home to confront her, but as time wore on into the afternoon she started to worry that he wouldn't even *try* to get her back. In fact, maybe she had played right into his hands by leaving, maybe he had reached the conclusion that he didn't want to be married any longer. For a male as rich and gorgeous as Rio the grass always had to look greener on the *single* side of the fence.

What had she done in walking out like that? What way was that to save a marriage?

She *loved* him, for goodness' sake, even if it turned out that he was the biggest flirt imaginable!

Suddenly feeling distinctly nauseous for the first time in her pregnancy, and shaky and damp with nerves, Ellie went upstairs to lie down. She knew the stress was bad for her and her baby and she beat herself up more for the decision she had made. Since when had she been a drama queen? And walking out on the assumption that the man you were leaving would follow to beg you to return was almost suicidal if he didn't love you.

Tears prickled and stung behind Ellie's lowered eyelids. What had persuaded her that she had to make such a theatrical challenge to Rio of all people? A fit of temporary insanity?

Rio walked through the bedroom door and surveyed his wife. She was fast asleep and his keen gaze could detect the faint redness round her eyes that suggested tears had been shed. His confidence rose. If his unemotional Ellie had been crying, that was a healthy sign. He sat down on the side of the bed and gently shook her shoulder.

Luminous green eyes flew open and settled on him in strained silence. Her lush lips parted and closed again as she regrouped and sat up to hug her knees. 'What are you doing here?' she asked coolly.

'You're here,' Rio said simply.

'You can't stay here,' Ellie argued, thoroughly disconcerted by that declaration. 'It's Beppe's house.'

'It's not. I bought it from him years ago when the upkeep was becoming too much for him. I begged him to stay on and look after it,' he explained with a casual shrug. 'It was a property investment for me—'

'You're such a liar!' Ellie told him helplessly. 'You did it because you love him!'

'That too.' Rio looked uncomfortable. 'Can we get to the point of what that stupid note you left behind meant? One sentence? I get *one* sentence of explanation?'

Ellie stiffened, more challenged than she had expected because Rio wasn't shouting or raging, giving her the fight she had subconsciously craved and yet feared with every atom of her being, lest it lead to the end of their relationship. She lowered her legs and slid off the other side of the bed. 'After the way you spent your morning, I should think the note was self-explanatory...'

'After the way I spent... Franca? You *saw* me with Franca?' Rio thundered without warning as he finally made the connection. 'Why the hell didn't you rescue me?'

Taken aback, Ellie froze. '*Rescue* you?'

'*Sì*...I'm sitting in a public place while a woman weeps and sobs and talks about the kind of stuff

I really don't want to know and I can't *decently* escape!' Rio recounted wrathfully. 'You think I was enjoying that? Are you out of your mind?'

It began to sink in on Ellie that she could have made a huge error of judgement.

'I can't believe this is all about Franca!' Rio exclaimed with rampant incredulity.

'You were holding hands. I thought you were flirting with her—'

'You need to learn what flirting entails, *principessa*. I assure you that there was no flirting whatsoever. Franca lost her eldest daughter to leukaemia only weeks ago and has only recently returned to work after compassionate leave.'

'Oh, my goodness...' Ellie whispered in shock. 'That poor, poor woman.'

'Yes, even Rio with the heart of a stone was not going to get up and walk away from that!' Rio grated. 'And that was only a part of the doom and gloom rehash of the previous nine years that took place. She said it did her good to get it off her conscience but it only made me realise that my sense of moral superiority over events back then was entirely unmerited.'

Ellie nodded. 'Okay. You contributed to the breakup and her going off with your business partner. I assumed that some of it must've been your fault.'

Rio dealt her an exasperated look. 'I *didn't*. I blamed Franca and Jax, but then I didn't know what was going on behind the scenes. Her fling with Jax only lasted about five minutes, and at her lowest ebb she ended up homeless.'

Feeling guiltier than ever for her wrong assumptions, Ellie backed down into a corner armchair and sighed. 'That can't have been easy for you to hear—'

Rio's gaze was sombre. 'No, even at the time I never wished harm on her, but then she lived with me and I didn't even realise I was living with an alcoholic—'

Ellie's brows lifted in wonderment.

Rio grimaced. 'That tells you how much attention I gave Franca. My sole interest back then was really the business of making money. But to some extent that wasn't *all* my fault. I was driven by the need to show Franca's family that I could provide well for her. They had done everything they could to try to separate us—'

Ellie was now genuinely interested in what he was telling her and some of her stress had ebbed because she had recognised that her worst fears had been groundless. 'But why?'

'Primarily my background,' Rio divulged stiffly.

'That you grew up as an orphan?' Ellie exclaimed. 'But that's so unfair!'

Rio braced himself to tell the truth and he paled and gritted his teeth. 'It was more sordid than that. I was an abandoned baby, born addicted to heroin. I was left in a cardboard box in a dumpster and found by street cleaners,' he admitted very stiffly. 'The manufacturer's name on the box was Rio. The nuns christened me Jerome after St Jerome but I was always known as Rio.'

Ellie was so appalled that she couldn't speak. She glanced away to get herself back under control but her eyes shone with shocked tears. To think of Rio as a defenceless baby thrown out like so much rubbish absolutely broke her heart. 'Why…a dumpster? Why not somewhere safer?'

'I asked my mother when I met her. She said she didn't want to get in trouble or be asked questions. It was nothing to do with my safety—it was *all* to do with her. I meant nothing to her. She was an addict and a whore,' he confessed grimly. 'Franca's family were convinced that I had to have evil genes. Some people *do* think like that, Ellie, which is why I've always kept the circumstances of my birth a secret. It is not that I am ashamed but that I do not wish to be pitied or thought of as being a lesser person because of those circumstances.'

Fierce protectiveness slivered through Ellie as she looked back at him, all the love she had for him enveloping her. 'I love you no matter what you came from. I love you more than I've ever loved anyone or anything and I *like* Rio as a name. And only now understanding why it was so important for you to give our child a safer, happier start in life…well, it only makes me love you even more!'

Rio was transfixed. He had been prepared for Ellie to flinch and be repulsed by the sleazy facts of his birth and ancestry and then pretend that they didn't matter even when it was obvious that they did. He certainly hadn't expected her to tell him that she loved him without reservation.

'Don't you realise,' she murmured gruffly, her throat thickening, so great was her emotion, 'that you should be *proud* of what you've achieved from such a tough beginning in life? It genuinely makes me feel incredibly proud of you.'

Rio studied her, lustrous dark golden eyes with a suspicious shine, lean, darkly handsome face clenched hard. 'You mean…all that?'

Ellie rose from her seat, empowered by his stillness, his uncharacteristic uncertainty. Never had she loved him more or understood him better. Franca and her family had taught him to be ashamed of his birth and background and she marvelled at their unwitting cruelty over something that he could not have influenced as she crossed the room and wrapped both arms tightly round him.

'Hug time?' Rio interpreted shakily, hoping she didn't catch the break in his voice, because in his whole life he had never known such a relief as the moment when Ellie told him that she *loved* him no matter what. It was the unconditional love he had sought without ever knowing it and suddenly he didn't feel alone and pitched against the world any longer.

'Hug time,' Ellie confirmed unevenly, winding round him like a vine. 'I'm really sorry I misunderstood what I saw with you and Franca. I sort of went haywire. I knew she was your first love and I thought maybe—'

'No.' Rio shuddered at the thought. 'She's happily married to a radiographer at the hospital and has two other children. But she developed a guilt complex about me when she finally got into rehab and started to rebuild her life. She says part of the recovery therapy was the need to mend fences with those she had wronged while she was still drinking but she could never face getting in touch with me after what she had done.'

'So, when she met you again—'

'It all came spilling out.' Rio sighed heavily. 'And I *had* to listen. It would have been cruel to tell her that it was very old history for me and that I no longer cared. I kept on saying that we had both made mistakes and weren't suited in any case but she kept on and on and on talking and crying—'

'I'm glad I didn't interrupt. Listening was the right thing to do. That was kind because I'm sure you were very uncomfortable and if I could've seen your face, I would've known that, but I could only see *her* face. When did you become that sensitive without me noticing?' Ellie asked in honest surprise.

'Oh, that probably happened when I realised I was in love with you. I then decided that I wanted to be the perfect husband—'

'You are…but I'm a very imperfect, distrustful wife,' Ellie mumbled in shame, burying her hot face in his shoulder, drinking in the familiar scent of him with an enormous sense of relief combined with sheer wonderment. He *loved* her? Her gorgeous, passion-filled, outrageously exciting husband loved her? He didn't find her too boring or sensible? Jealous and possessive? She was ecstatic with wondering happiness. 'So what happened with your mother when you did meet her?'

'There was a piece in the newspaper about me being found when I was abandoned and she always knew where I was. When I began to make money she looked me up,' he confided grimly. 'And that's all she wanted... Money. She told me a lot of lies. I found out that although she had weaned herself off her own addiction, she made a living by dealing drugs to others. I had nothing more to do with her—'

'That must have hurt.' Ellie sighed in sympathy.

'It is what it is. Getting off drugs didn't magically turn her into a nice or caring woman.' Rio shrugged. 'As to my potential father? I was an accident. Probably one of her customers. She had no idea.'

'It really doesn't matter to me,' Ellie emphasised. 'I wasn't only saying that. What matters to me is the man you are now and I love him. I even love you a little more for being kind to Franca, which you must've found trying.'

Rio tilted up her face, dark golden eyes adoring. 'There could never be another woman for me, Ellie. I've never loved like this. I didn't know I even *could* love like this but you're everything I ever wanted in a woman...even if I didn't realise that until I met you the second time.'

'We just fought,' Ellie groaned.

'And I got more of a kick out of fighting with you than I got out of any affair I've ever had,' Rio confessed. 'But the hunger for you was overwhelming...I couldn't fight that—'

Ellie lifted warm eyes to his lean, strong face, glorying in his scorching appraisal. 'I couldn't either. I always keep my feet firmly on the ground and then I met you and everything, including me, went crazy—'

'But we've had so much enjoyment out of each other,' Rio commented with appreciation. 'On levels I didn't even know there could be between a man and a woman. Before you, it was all about sex for me—'

'Oh, I know that.' Ellie flushed. 'In Dharia—'

Rio winced. 'I was a jerk...but I had never wanted any woman the way I wanted you that night and I was on a high and then it all went pear-shaped, thanks to the twins—'

'Perhaps we both needed another couple of years to be ready for something more serious,' Ellie suggested forgivingly.

'*Dio mio*, I love you!' Rio swore passionately in receipt of the face-saving, utterly unearned excuse she was giving him and appreciating her generosity. He gathered her into his arms and almost squeezed her with his enthusiasm into suffocation. 'Really, *really* love you and I can't wait for the baby now that I know for sure that I have you by my side...'

'Well, when you ordered that giant train set in Venice and told me there was no reason why a little girl shouldn't enjoy it as much as a little boy I kind of guessed that our baby would be welcomed,' Ellie confided as he smoothly edged her down onto the bed. 'Nap time for pregnant Ellie, is it?'

'No. No rest for the imperfect wife,' Rio teased with a charismatic slashing grin as he looked down at her flushed, smiling face. 'Adriano was so relieved when you and then I showed up. He hates the house being empty because he has nothing to do and he's been fretting about Beppe. He's making dinner for seven, which gives us a few hours to fill—'

Ellie's eyes widened at that implication. 'You mean, you were so sure of yourself when you arrived here that you just went ahead and ordered dinner?' she exclaimed in disbelief.

'I wasn't prepared to leave here without you and if you refused to leave I had a case out in the car to enable me to stay here with you,' Rio explained without hesitation. 'When I want something, *principessa*...I don't quit and I don't surrender and I do believe that I would fight to the death to keep you in my life.'

'At heart you're a romantic,' Ellie told him with

satisfaction and approval. 'When I came here, I was fighting for you too—'

Rio interrupted her in Italian to tell her argumentatively that walking out of their marital home had been a dreadful, shocking action to take.

Ellie refused to apologise. 'I was trying to make a statement, draw a line for you. Maybe it was a little extreme but I was hurting so badly—'

'I don't need a damn line, woman... I've got you in the flesh!' Rio told her aggressively. 'And it was not only extreme but also forbidden. You are not allowed to walk out on me ever again in this lifetime!'

'Is that a fact?'

'*Sì*... You're my wife, the centre of my world, my everything. You don't walk out. You stay and *shout.*'

Ellie breathed in deep, helplessly touched by that instruction. 'I'll shout the next time,' she promised.

'There won't *be* a next time!' Rio spelled out feelingly. 'Promise me—'

'*Sì*...I can promise that,' Ellie whispered, running adoring fingers through his cropped black hair and down one proud cheekbone to rest against his wilful lower lip. 'You're mine. I'm never going to walk away from you again.'

'Or drive off in my sports car,' Rio instructed. 'It's far too fast and powerful on these roads when you're not used to it.'

'I liked it—'

'No. I want you safe, *bella mia.*'

And before Ellie could demand that she had the right to influence what *he* drove in the interests of *his* safety, Rio kissed her with all the passion of his relief, love and desire for her and her impressionable toes curled. *Take that, sensible Dr Ellie*, she thought in wonderment that he truly was hers after all her anxiety and distrust, and then a thought occurred and she wrenched her mouth free...

'You never apologised for calling me a gold-digger!' she reminded him hotly.

'Of course I didn't.' Rio slowly shook his handsome dark head in apparent amazement at that reminder. 'That would have been owning up to flawed judgement or stupidity and it would've made you think less of me, so I decided to tough it out because I was trying to win you over to wanting to keep me by that stage.'

'*Nothing* would make me think less of you, you stupid man,' Ellie mumbled before she locked her lips to his again, his instant forgiveness procured, and there was no further conversation or indeed argument for quite some time. The excitement of their reconciliation powered the passion and the promises with buoyant happiness and fresh appreciation of the love they had found where they least expected it.

EPILOGUE

POLLY GROANED. 'I'M OUT of my depth here. What
do we do about this situation?'

Ellie groaned too. 'Mind our own business for
now. If the sister we haven't even met has a thoroughly wicked and dishonest father, it's not our
place to tell her so. Lucy doesn't know us or trust
us yet. She's found her dad and, at the very least,
probably thinks very highly of him and, at worst,
really loves him because he's been kind to her—'

'But what if he's just using her for some reason?' Polly proclaimed emotively. 'Doesn't she
deserve to know he went to prison for fraud?'

'We need to establish a relationship with her as
sisters first,' Ellie opined, crossing the terrace of
her Italian home to prevent her fiery little daughter from striking the younger prince of Dharia,
tall, sturdy Hassan, aged two, for taking one of

her dolls and wheeling his toy tractor over the top of it with little-boy glee.

Across the terrace, his older brother, Karim, the crown prince of Dharia, shouted at his little brother in Arabic.

'He's telling him off,' Polly translated. 'He's so like Rashad, very well behaved.'

'That's never going to be my problem with Teresina,' Ellie whispered. 'She's always ready to fight for what she wants. It's a continual battle.'

'Well, you mix two pretty opinionated people like you and Rio and that's what you get,' Polly pointed out cheerfully. 'She's gorgeous with that hair though.'

Ellie smiled at her daughter, who was two years old now. Born of parents who both had curly hair, Teresina had miraculously straight shoulder-length black hair and eyes that were a lighter green than her mother's. She was small and slight in build and had learned to walk at nine months old. She was lively and quick-tempered and the greatest joy in Ellie's world, for she had never realised just how much she would love her child.

In the three years that Ellie had been married, her whole life had changed and she had not a single regret. She spoke fluent Italian and had secured her dream job in the hospital where Beppe had been treated and where she was now continuing her training as a doctor specialising in children's ailments. Beppe had made an excellent recovery and had, under considerable protest, begun walking to take exercise. She had grown very close to her father and was profoundly grateful to have found him in time to get to know him.

They had finally contrived to trace their long-lost sister to Greece, where she was living with her birth father, who appeared to be a most unsavoury man. But Ellie was convinced that considerable tact had to be utilised where their unknown sister was concerned and Polly and Ellie had yet to work out how to best approach Lucy without frightening her off. Ellie was in favour of sending the ruby ring with a letter introducing themselves and inviting contact. How that would go down was anyone's guess but at least it couldn't be seen as threatening or interfering.

Ellie had grown no keener on shopping in recent years, because if she wasn't at work she was exulting in precious *family* time and certainly didn't want to waste that time shopping and preening. Ellie had always dressed for comfort and she was still doing it. For that reason, Polly was still buying her clothes and now Rio was doing it too and her wardrobe was bursting at the seams with designer garments she only wore at the occasional swanky event Rio attended. On the jewellery front, however, her collection could almost have rivalled the jewellery of Dharia's royal family. Rio never went anywhere and came back without gifts for her and Teresina, and soon he would have a third little person to buy for, Ellie thought with quiet contentment. And she had finally told her sister the story of their grandmother's diamond brooch and Polly had simply laughed and dismissed the matter without concern, more worried that Ellie had had to deal with their uncle's spite without support.

The sound of a car coming down the drive sent Ellie leaping upright.

'I'll watch the kids,' Polly proffered. 'Go on… greet him and make his day! Rio's so romantic.'

Rashad climbed out of the passenger seat. The friendship he and Rio had formed while at university had only deepened when the men married sisters who liked to see each other regularly.

Rio's sizzling smile broke out as Ellie threw herself at him and wrapped her arms round his neck as if she hadn't seen him in a week. He was a little disconcerted because he had only left her early that morning and she wasn't usually given to any public displays of affection.

'You missed me?' he whispered, wondering if something was worrying her.

'A little. I've got news,' Ellie murmured soft and low. 'Let's go upstairs.'

'Is this about your sister Lucy?'

'No, nothing new there. Polly still wants to jump in the royal jet and land on Lucy's doorstep and explode into her life,' Ellie told him ruefully. 'But I think she's beginning to come round to a more diplomatic approach.'

As Rashad, the king of Dharia, strolled past

them to join his wife and two sons Ellie gripped Rio's hand and practically dragged him up to their bedroom.

'You're beginning to worry me,' Rio confided, shooting a glance at Ellie's glowing face and registering that whatever had happened, it couldn't be anything bad.

'We're pregnant again!' Ellie announced with delight.

Rio blinked and nodded very slowly. 'I wasn't aware we were even *trying...*'

'I didn't want to put pressure on you so I didn't mention that I wasn't taking anything,' Ellie revealed cheerfully.

Rio almost laughed out loud. *Put pressure on him?* Nothing could keep him away from Ellie. He adored her. But he still compressed his lips and said, 'It might have been nice to be asked... to have discussed this as a couple,' he remarked, rather woodenly because he still wanted to laugh.

Ellie's face fell as if he'd slapped it. 'I didn't think of that. I know how much you love having Teresina and I want to have my family while I'm still young and I would like them close together in age.' She chewed uncomfortably at her lower lip. 'I suppose I should've said something—'

Rio grinned. 'I was only joking. I'm delighted,' he assured her with heartfelt enthusiasm. 'The more the merrier—'

'Polly's pregnant again too. She's very keen to have a daughter,' she confided. 'I'll tell her about me over dinner, so don't go breaking my news ahead of me like you did the last time with that phone call.'

Rio linked his arms round her slim waist. 'It's my news too, *principessa*. I did figure in the conception.'

Ellie beamed up at him approvingly. 'Yes, you're wonderfully fertile—'

'Good to know I'm useful for something—'

'*And* spectacularly good at the action part,' Ellie whispered lovingly, hands running below his jacket to skate possessively over his hard muscled chest and then lowering in a much more intimate caress.

Rio shed his jacket and his shirt in record time.

'I won't sulk about not being consulted on the extending-the-family issue,' he admitted huskily. 'I know Dr Ellie was in the driving seat worrying that I might suffer from performance anxiety in bed for the first time in my life. In short, I'm perfectly happy to be used and useful.'

'I know you are,' Ellie told him cheerfully, shimmying out of her dress even faster, her eyes full of love and appreciation as she fasted her gaze on his lean, bronzed body, the passion that always simmered below the surface of their marriage gripping both of them with its scorching intensity. 'Did I ever tell you how much I love you?'

'Not since last night.' Rio studied his wife with wondering admiration and marvelled that he had found her, that she had married him, learned to love him and overlooked his every flaw. Loving Ellie had brought him untold riches in the happiness stakes and he would never ever take it for granted because he had lived too long without that security. 'But if you want to be competitive, you couldn't possibly love me as much as I love you...'

* * * * *

If you enjoyed this
BRIDES FOR THE TAKING *story,*
don't forget to read the first part of the trilogy
THE DESERT KING'S BLACKMAILED BRIDE
Available now!

Also, look out for these other great
Lynne Graham reads!
THE GREEK'S CHRISTMAS BRIDE
THE ITALIAN'S CHRISTMAS CHILD
BOUGHT FOR THE GREEK'S REVENGE
THE SICILIAN'S STOLEN SON
Available now!

MILLS & BOON®
Large Print – August 2017

The Italian's One-Night Baby
Lynne Graham

The Desert King's Captive Bride
Annie West

Once a Moretti Wife
Michelle Smart

The Boss's Nine-Month Negotiation
Maya Blake

The Secret Heir of Alazar
Kate Hewitt

Crowned for the Drakon Legacy
Tara Pammi

His Mistress with Two Secrets
Dani Collins

Stranded with the Secret Billionaire
Marion Lennox

Reunited by a Baby Bombshell
Barbara Hannay

The Spanish Tycoon's Takeover
Michelle Douglas

Miss Prim and the Maverick Millionaire
Nina Singh

MILLS & BOON®
Large Print – September 2017

The Sheikh's Bought Wife
Sharon Kendrick

The Innocent's Shameful Secret
Sara Craven

The Magnate's Tempestuous Marriage
Miranda Lee

The Forced Bride of Alazar
Kate Hewitt

Bound by the Sultan's Baby
Carol Marinelli

Blackmailed Down the Aisle
Louise Fuller

Di Marcello's Secret Son
Rachael Thomas

Conveniently Wed to the Greek
Kandy Shepherd

His Shy Cinderella
Kate Hardy

Falling for the Rebel Princess
Ellie Darkins

Claimed by the Wealthy Magnate
Nina Milne

MILLS & BOON®

Why shop at millsandboon.co.uk?

Each year, thousands of romance readers find their perfect read at millsandboon.co.uk. That's because we're passionate about bringing you the very best romantic fiction. Here are some of the advantages of shopping at www.millsandboon.co.uk:

* **Get new books first**—you'll be able to buy your favourite books one month before they hit the shops

* **Get exclusive discounts**—you'll also be able to buy our specially created monthly collections, with up to 50% off the RRP

* **Find your favourite authors**—latest news, interviews and new releases for all your favourite authors and series on our website, plus ideas for what to try next

* **Join in**—once you've bought your favourite books, don't forget to register with us to rate, review and join in the discussions

Visit **www.millsandboon.co.uk**
for all this and more today!